FATAL CHARM

FATAL CHARM

Anne Morice

St. Martin's Press
New York

Library of Congress Cataloging-in-Publication Data

Morice, Anne.
       Fatal charm / Anne Morice.
                p.   cm.
       ISBN 0-312-03338-9
     I. Title.
   PR6063.O743F38   1989
   823'.914—dc20   89-30510
                                                                   CIP

First published in Great Britain by Macmillan London Limited.

First U.S. Edition

10   9   8   7   6   5   4   3   2   1

FATAL CHARM

ONE

Being a party to someone else's secret is something I try to avoid. Fearful of breaking my Trappist vows through forgetfulness, or for some less laudable reason, I tend to lock the information away in the dark recesses of my mind and then lose the key. But this is a poor solution. To be unaware of possessing a secret can, as I have discovered to my cost, lead to as much trouble as betraying it.

Marriage, in this respect as in so many others, has been a great blessing, since sharing a confidence with Robin is the nearest equivalent to lowering it forty fathoms deep on to the ocean bed and whispering it to a drowsy mollusc. On the other hand, since this is the only resemblance he bears to such a creature and can be relied upon to bring the subject up from time to time in the privacy of our own apartments, it remains exactly as it should be, alive but quiescent.

These attributes, granted to him by nature, have been refined and developed during his career at the CID and have doubtless contributed to his steady promotion to the rank of Chief Inspector and they have often proved invaluable to me on a less exalted level. By a curious coincidence, however, on more than one occasion, some seemingly trivial piece of gossip or information which has

7

been passed on to him in this way has eventually landed up in the files of New Scotland Yard.

There appeared to be no such threat hanging over the story which I related to him one evening a few months ago. It arose from the fact that I had been prevailed upon by my agent, more or less at gun point, to take part in one of those television surprise tributes to a celebrated figure of our time, which are so dear to the hearts of television companies and their accountants.

'What have accountants got to do with it?' Robin asked.

'Pretty well everything. Do you mean to tell me you've never watched "Birthday Tribute"?'

'Only when it was called Trooping the Colour.'

'Oh no, nothing like that. This is just some cheese-paring studio production which goes out once a month to honour some celebrity or other. It's usually an actor because they're so much better at pretending to be bowled over by surprise than most amateurs and it must be one of the cheapest fifty-minute shows ever devised. No writers, no costumes, only one set and a cast of dozens, who don't get paid a penny, apart from expenses.'

'A kind of glorified chat show, by the sound of it. Who's the lucky victim this time?'

'Evadne Proctor, equally well known as Lady Deverell. I suppose one of those names conveys something to you?'

'Yes, indeed! Wasn't she the old girl who was in that play you did at Bath last year?'

'The same, only she might not have described our separate contributions in quite that way.'

'And wife of the old barnstormer, Hartley Deverell?'

'Widow. He toppled downstairs during one of his drinking bouts a few months ago and no one seemed to notice, so he died of exposure, or maybe frustration. You're doing very well, Robin.'

'And I haven't finished either. I seem to recall a number

of offspring who are also well known in your world. Is that right?'

'Yes, not to mention an assortment of grandchildren waiting on tiptoe in the wings.'

'So what is there for you to worry about?'

'Plenty, I should have thought. Your knowing so much about them confirms my theory that most other people in this country are equally well informed.'

'But you're not asking me to believe that a brood like that wouldn't brief the mother hen in advance about every move in the game? I can't see them leaving anything to chance where their public image is concerned.'

'Neither can I. Candida will see to that, but it's not the old lady herself who bothers me.'

'Who, then?'

'Well, you see, Robin, it's estimated that up to twelve million viewers tune into this programme, mainly out of curiosity. A large proportion of them get hooked in the first two minutes and stay with it, even when they've discovered the birthday boy or girl is someone they've never heard of, or actively dislike. But, if they knew this in advance, more than half of them wouldn't bother to switch on in the first place, so it's of the highest importance that the cat should remain in the bag until the very last second. Quite apart from my honour being at stake and although I only have a tiny part, hardly more than a walk on, I wouldn't want them to miss that, as well. That's why I've told you. It's a kind of safety valve.'

'How flattering! And how long will you have to hold out with the rest of the world? When does this event take place?'

'Monday evening, which means that I shall have to be particularly on my guard at the weekend, when we're staying with Toby.'

'Oh, I shouldn't think you'd have much to worry about

9

there. Admittedly, your cousin Toby is not the most discreet of men, but he's unlikely to be touched by anything so far removed from his own concerns and he certainly never watches television, so far as I know.'

'Maybe not, but Mrs Parkes does, and she'd be certain to choose that moment to bring the potatoes in. She does so love being in the know ahead of everyone else and, in her prim and supercilious way, she'd manage to spread the news round the entire neighbourhood in less time than it takes her to scramble an egg. Not forgetting to name the source either, and that would really fix me. Come to think of it, though, I might tell Ellen. She's another like the grave and not a great television watcher, so she'd be almost certain to miss it.'

'Will Ellen be there this weekend too?'

'Yes, but without Jeremy, you may be relieved to hear. I know it must have come as a great relief to Toby.'

'They haven't parted, have they?'

'Oh, my goodness, no. That is, only temporarily. Jeremy's in New York on one of those business trips he's so keen about. That's why Ellen thought that, rather than stay alone and forlorn in London, she'd spend the weekend with us. I'll tell her about "Birthday Tribute" in muffled undertones as we stroll on a deserted part of the Common. It will have a special interest for her because one of Jeremy's sisters is married to a cousin of Eliza Deverell's husband, if you can work all that out.'

'I could, if I considered it necessary, but in fact Eliza Deverell is a new one on me. I've never heard of her. Is she an actress too?'

'Not any more. She's Evadne's youngest child and the only one of them to opt out. Like all the others, she was shoved on to the stage at the age of sixteen, but she hated it and a year or two afterwards she ran off and married an anthropologist. They now live on some godforsaken island in the Pacific, so remote and primitive that you have to do the shopping in Australia, as far as I can gather.'

'So she won't be taking part in this celebration?'

'Not in person. They have a two-minute film clip of her, shot in Sydney, saying that she would give the whole world to be there on this day of days, telling everyone that Evadne is the loveliest Mum ever and blowing kisses to one and all, and that suits Candida down to the ground.'

'Does it? Why's that?'

'Because she'll have enough competition to fight off as it is, and the story goes that, although Eliza chucked it in, she actually had more natural talent than the rest of the bunch put together. Great personality and bursting with charm too, from all one hears, with a sense of humour thrown in, which is a rare commodity in that family. So far as Candida is concerned, no Pacific island could be too remote for her baby sister.'

'Sounds like a jolly evening. What does your tiny part consist of?'

'About one and a half minutes. I should explain that the studio is a converted theatre, complete with packed auditorium, and the stage is set as for a cocktail party for twenty or thirty people. Several of the guests, myself included, are already assembled and the boy behind the bar turns out to be one of the grandsons. At this point, enter Evadne, with the master of ceremonies at her side and Candida as a sort of train bearer. Not until two minutes earlier, when she came out of the make-up room, had she the tiniest inkling of what was in store. She believed that she was there to take part in some ordinary, run-of-the-mill chat show. That's the theory, anyway. Once on, she's installed in a sort of throne-like armchair and the remaining guests start to arrive. Each of us goes in pre-arranged order to pay homage and rattle off a line or two. In my case, it's the "Do you remember" theme. "Do you remember, Evadne," I say,

11

"the night when Hero went on instead of you and nearly stole the show?" Whereupon, if her reflexes are properly tuned up, she bursts into gales of happy, non-committal laughter and I turn to the presenter and reel off a largely apocryphal anecdote about her beastly little King Charles spaniel, which escaped from her dressing room one evening and found its way on to the stage. It's name is Hero, as you've doubtless gathered. Not even the animals in that family have escaped being named after some character in whatever play the old boy was appearing in when they arrived. It's lucky for them that no one was born during the run of *Coriolanus*.'

'So what do you all do after that?'

'Oh well, Evadne presumably makes whatever response she was able to dream up while I was gushing on and I then retire to my place in the crowd. And that's my lot. The show has to struggle on without me for another twenty minutes.'

'Well, I'll make a point of watching it, providing I get home in time. And we could meet for dinner afterwards, if you like. I don't suppose you'll feel in the mood for cooking.'

'No, but the thing is— ' I said.

'What thing?'

'They're laying on a party afterwards for the company and cast in a private room at the New Westminster. You're invited, naturally, but I've warned them that you may not be able to make it. All the same, it would be a great help to me if you could and, anyway, why should we pay for dinner when there's a free one on offer?'

I could tell that the last argument did not carry much weight and that it had probably been a mistake to include it, for he said, 'I should think I'd be more of a hindrance than a help. I shan't know a soul and I shouldn't have the remotest idea what to say to them if I did.'

'You'd provide moral support for me, which is what counts. Do try and come, if you can.'

'Oh, if you say so. I'll see how things work out and give you a call at lunchtime,' he replied and I left it at that. Some ideas need a while to be chewed on and digested.

TWO

< 1 >

It was Ellen who provided the postscript, and a fairly
baffling one it was.

Now in her early twenties, Ellen is the only child by
the first of his two disastrous marriages, of my cousin
Toby, who lives at Roakes Common in Oxfordshire and
who occasionally finds the energy or, as he would put
it, time to hammer out a light comedy, each of which
has found favour with the theatre-going public, despite
a certain flavour of cynicism.

Being approximately midway in age between them,
I could easily have found myself in the uncomfortable
role of buffer state, used by each and inevitably earning
the dislike of both. Fortunately, though, apart from the
little matter of Toby's unrelenting prejudice against his
son-in-law, Jeremy Roxburgh, which Ellen is both well
aware of and perfectly unmoved by, they are the best of
friends and no buffering is required.

On that Sunday morning she and I were seated in garden
chairs beside the swimming pool, without a soul in sight or
earshot. Robin had gone to the golf club, Mrs Parkes was
in the kitchen, concocting delicious dishes for lunch and
Toby had declared his intention of spending the morning

upstairs, grappling with the current play and, presumably, in view of their conspicuous absence, combing the Sunday papers for inspiration to spur him on.

Seizing my chance, I had spent the previous ten minutes telling Ellen of the so-called surprise tribute for Evadne's eightieth birthday.

'So that probably accounts for it,' she remarked when I had come to the bit about Eliza, and then proceeded to explain this apparent *non sequitur* by asking, 'You remember Jeremy's sister, Venetia?'

'I remember she was one of your bridesmaids, but I haven't seen her since.'

'She's being very coy and secretive at the moment.'

'What about?'

'I couldn't make out. She's married to a Harley Street specialist and they live in Windsor now, where he has some kind of clinic, but we were both lunching with her mother yesterday. There were some other women there as well, and one of them invited Venetia to do something or other next week. She went into a wild tizz and said she was most frantically sorry, but she couldn't make any plans at all for next week and we'd never guess, but – and then she clapped her hands to her mouth and started to giggle and say something like, "Ooops, there I go again and it's supposed to be a deathly secret." So all is now clear. She must be appearing in the programme too.'

'What on earth would they want her for?'

'Oh well, you know, her father was given a peerage, as a reward for working so hard to make all his millions and I expect that gives her a certain cachet. Besides, she's forever boasting about the Deverell connection, even though we all know it's only some remote cousin of her husband's who's married to Eliza. Venetia always pretends to know her a lot better than she really does and I suppose the television people have fallen for it.'

'I rather doubt that, you know, Ellen. They have a huge research department, headed by none other than Joan Manders-Hobson, burrowing away on that kind of thing and it would only need one or two pertinent questions, like "When did you last see your husband's cousin's wife?" Besides, you said she wasn't accepting invitations for the whole week and, if she's really been invited to the party, she must know that it's tomorrow, which leaves six clear days. And, in case you want any more, it's not a programme about Eliza. She's more or less in the same position as I am, just a cog in Evadne's wheel. So what would they need Venetia for?'

'No, they wouldn't, would they? So I must have got it wrong and it was something else she was being coy about. Want me to find out? I don't foresee much difficulty in getting it out of her.'

'Why bother, though, since it's unlikely to be of the faintest interest to anyone but herself?'

'It was such a strange coincidence, that's what annoys me,' Ellen said.

'I'm with you there. Strange coincidences which turn out to have no significance are always annoying. One is nagged by the feeling of having overlooked something.'

< 2 >

'Did you ever have a Deverell in one of your plays?' I asked Toby during lunch.

'I wonder if Mrs Parkes is about to bring the potatoes?' Robin remarked in a dreamy voice.

'It's all right,' I told him, 'it won't matter whether she does or not. This is something else. Did you hear what I said, Toby?'

16

'I heard what both of you said and, taking them one at a time, there are plenty of potatoes on the sideboard already and I see nothing to stop Robin helping himself.'

'Never mind about that, it was only a private joke. What's the other answer?'

'I suppose, in a manner of speaking, it is yes and no.'

'What manner of speaking would that be?'

'Some idiot got the idea a few years ago of reviving *Pieces of Eight*, which was the second play I wrote and very bad, even in its day. They sent it out on a pre-London tour, with Evadne playing Constance, but it never got further than Guildford. A most misguided venture, from start to finish. Cheap production, shoddy sets, next to illiterate director and third-rate cast. Why does everyone keep talking about the Deverells these days?'

'I've noticed that, too,' Ellen said. 'I suppose it is the kind of thing that goes in waves. Don't you agree, Robin?'

'Maybe, although it would need to be a pretty powerful wave to have washed up on Roakes, I should imagine.'

'You are mistaken, dear boy, Roakes is where it started. And please understand that by everyone I refer to Mrs Parkes. How would I know what people in general are talking about? I find it hard enough at my own table.'

'So, having cleared that up,' I said, 'what does Mrs Parkes say everyone else is saying?'

'That those dreadful Clarkes have sold their cowman's cottage for a hefty sum to a member of the Deverell clan.'

'You don't say! Not Candida?'

'No, one of the granddaughters. Rosie, I believe she's called.'

'Oh, Benedick's daughter. He's got two, but I can't remember whether Rosie is the unmarried one with a child, or the married one without.'

'The former, presumably, since she goes under the name of Deverell and her gentleman friend is called Mr

17

something else. There is also a child on the premises. You can imagine Mrs Parkes's reaction to that. She says it is the kind of thing that may go down well in Chelsea, but won't do for Roakes. I can't for one moment think what she is talking about, since at least half the children in this village were born out of wedlock. However, she has one law for the natives and another for the foreign invaders. When she runs out of moral objections, she has the audacity to tell us that it doesn't matter two hoots to her what grown-up people do with their lives, it's that poor kiddie that worries her.'

'Have you met this Rosie, Toby?'

'No, and I have no wish to. Her hair is like scrambled egg and she is dressed in rejects from the jumble sale. The young man is equally unattractive, although he appears to be devoted to the child, even though we are told he is not the father. He wears it strapped on to himself like a chest protector. Which reminds me, I hope it's not going to rain this afternoon and spoil our game of croquet.'

'Your Dad is not quite his usual sunny self today,' I remarked to Ellen, when we became isolated from the other two by their superior strength, skill and competitive spirit, 'or do I imagine it?'

'No, but at least it's not on account of Jeremy this time. He's probably reached a sticky patch with the play. On the other hand, perhaps he ought to see a psychiatrist.'

'Oh no, Ellen, you wouldn't wish that on your worst enemy,' I said, thinking of the poor psychiatrist. 'There must be easier ways of cheering him up. In the meantime, this is obviously no moment to break the news about Rosie Deverell.'

'Not if it's unpleasant, certainly, but you can tell me, if you like.'

'She's only about your age, but I'm told there have already been one or two meaningful relationships in her

18

life, all of them doomed from the start. She's a collector of lame ducks apparently and the current one, whose name is Brian, is not only frightful in all the usual ways, he also has a police record.'

'Go on! You mean he's done time?'

'I believe he got off in the end, but at one point he was hauled in for theft.'

'What had he stolen?'

'I've forgotten the details, but some well-heeled female had a lot of valuables pinched from her flat. Brian happened to have been staying there until the day before; or rather, he'd more or less dumped himself on her, apparently having turned up begging for refuge when he'd been turned out of his lodgings. The next morning she gave him some cash and told him to get fixed up with a room and pay her back when he'd sorted himself out. However, he had no luck and when she took charge of that, too, there was always some reason why the room she'd found for him wouldn't be suitable. Three weeks later he was still making himself at home in her flat, running up telephone bills, eating and drinking his way through all her supplies and generally making a disgusting nuisance of himself.'

'Couldn't she have found some rugger-playing hearty to boot him out?'

'No, she's not that sort. She has a heavy social conscience about the disadvantaged. Naturally, such women attract him like a magnet. However, this one finally did reach the end of her tether. She told him that her parents were coming to stay and it was essential that he should remove himself from the premises forthwith.'

'Did it work?'

'Up to a point. He must have believed her because when she arrived home from work that evening he'd gone, pausing only to pop a bottle or two and a few small but expensive items into his knapsack. Much to her relief,

19

however, since it had already struck her that it might be a smart move to get the lock changed, he had left her spare set of keys on the kitchen table.'

'Did it not occur to her that he might have had duplicates made?'

'I tell you, she's not like that. You and I, who've been brought up in a hard school, might have been suspicious, but this one trusts her fellow men, particularly if they happen to be cadgers and layabouts. Two days later, when her flat was burgled, she still refused to believe that Brian could have been responsible. I daresay that was partly because she felt guilty about having turned him out.'

'So he got away with it?'

'By a fluke. It turned out that there had been scaffolding outside the next-door building for several weeks and it would have been just possible for some athlete to have hauled himself up till he was on a level with her balcony and done a sort of Tarzan leap. And, after all, who are we to judge? Perhaps it did happen like that. All the same, it's not the kind of story to persuade Toby to take a kindly view of his new neighbours.'

'I agree, but what puzzles me, Tess, is how you always know about these things. How on earth did you come by that one?'

'Pure luck. It was due to a temporary crack in the Deverell façade during the run of *The Rivals* in Bath. Evadne had been rather misguidedly cast as Mrs Malaprop and she had had what they politely call mixed notices, which had dented her confidence a bit and then, not very long after we opened, Candida went off to make a film in California. I think that was the main trouble. She's the real dictator in that family and without her rod of iron the other members are always liable to lose their bearings. Anyway, the crunch came when Benedick went on a drinking bout and started breathing fire and brimstone about

Rosie's latest entanglement. Not content with saddling the family with a bastard child, she had now taken up with this criminal fiend, who was obviously seeking a comfortable existence at Benedick's expense and off they'd whipped to some squalid little shack in the remote countryside, which is the sort of contradiction in terms that always comes spluttering out of Benedick when he's in these moods. As a matter of fact, I'd assumed the squalid shack was in Wales, but that may have been because they nearly always are.'

'Perhaps they started in Wales, in the time-honoured fashion and then someone came and set fire to the shack and they had to move on?'

'Yes, most likely. Anyway, what with one thing and another, Evadne, stuck down in Bath and far from all her dear ones, lost her head and started pouring out her troubles to anyone who would listen, which meant that I got the brunt of it. The mood soon passed, of course. A day or two later she was back in her regal mould again, soldiering on with a merry twinkle.'

'Do you suppose Rosie has been invited to the birthday party?'

'As a matter of fact, she has. I picked up that bit from Joan Manders-Hobson, who is in charge of what they call the research. I suppose it would have looked bad if they'd left her out. However, Brian is definitely not on the guest list and Rosie on her own shouldn't cause too much mayhem.'

'Well, you're sure to have a captive audience in me,' Ellen said. 'I can't wait to see how they all conduct themselves.'

'Oh, I expect they'll be all right, they're pros, after all. Although, knowing them, I daresay they'll manage to spring a few surprises on us.'

THREE

< 1 >

My first concern when it was over was whether Ellen had
stuck it out to the end. If so, she must have felt rewarded
far beyond expectations, for the big bombshell was held
back for the last two minutes of the show, coming at the
very moment when the full complement of guests were
preparing to raise their glasses and burst into 'Happy
Birthday to YOU'. This provided a most agreeable surprise
for the audience and the exact reverse for the majority of
the players, in particular, as was evident from her stony
expression, for the hitherto imperturbable Candida.

There had been a minor contretemps a few minutes
before this, which others beside myself may have regarded
as a somewhat less embarrassing episode than was liable to
occur in this artificial atmosphere of organised sentiment
and *bonhomie* and to feel that, if it proved to be the only
hitch, we could count ourselves lucky.

Rosie, predictably, was the culprit. Brian had been left
at home, but she had brought a great-grandson to the
party, a lolling, sandy-haired infant, who spent most of the
transmission time wobbling about on his mother's hip.

There had been a lightning flash of hatred in Evadne's
eyes as this pair entered, unlikely to have been noticed
by anyone in the audience, for within seconds she had

rallied, darting forward and sweeping her granddaughter into a fond embrace. After which she made a few clucking noises at the baby and then stood blowing kisses to them both, before turning away to speak to someone else.

However, Rosie had not done with us yet and after three or four other characters had made their entrances and had their names and claims to celebrity announced in ringing tones, she had decided that her child was hungry. It had not given any intimation of this to the rest of us, nor, so far as I had been able to perceive, displayed a single flicker of animation of any kind since their arrival. Nevertheless, some signal must have passed between them because, with no warning, Rosie strode forward, planted herself in a chair downstage and transferred the child from her hip to the upper part of her anatomy.

Naturally, this was not a scene which any quick-thinking cameraman would have neglected to record, if only for the archives, but Candida's sixth or seventh sense had evidently alerted her just in time to foil him. Thinking simultaneously with her head, feet and hands, she moved to the piano and began gently and absent-mindedly picking out the opening bars of the Moonlight Sonata.

'Oh, do go on!' her mother entreated. 'It's my very favourite of all. It always makes me want to cry.'

This, in my opinion, showed admirable presence of mind, and daring too, since, knowing something of her taste in music, which more or less began and ended with the works of Ivor Novello, she was most unlikely to have been able to name that particular piece. Luckily, any risk of her being called upon to do so was obviated by the arrival at this point of two more guests.

Rosie having thus been out-manoeuvred, all then proceeded without a hitch until the moment when, as has been said, we were preparing ourselves for the final 'Ave, Evadne!' and the off-stage signal from the floor manager for the audience to start the applause. A split second later we subsided into total silence, as the double doors at the back of the stage were flung open yet again and on marched Eliza, grinning from ear to ear, looking as fresh as paint and somehow contriving, in her plain-looking slacks and shirt, to make every other woman present look overdressed or dowdy.

Mercifully, there were now only two minutes running time left, for, from that moment on, no one else got a look in and Rosie could have given birth to triplets, for all anyone would have noticed.

This *tour de force* on Eliza's part did not appear to spring from any conscious effort. It was simply that the legend had turned into reality and that she possessed some mysterious, life-enhancing quality which made her irresistible and as hard to divert the eye from as the aurora borealis. A truer word was never spoken than that, so far as Candida was concerned, no Pacific island could be too remote for her baby sister, Eliza.

< 2 >

'And that was a real blockbuster of a secret,' I told Robin in the taxi on our way to the New Westminster Hotel, 'I can only be thankful that it wasn't entrusted to me.'

'You mean no one at all knew she was going to turn up? Not even her family?'

'Least of all her family. One glance at their faces was enough to show that. It made you realise that, after all, there's a slight but subtle difference between being dumb-founded and acting dumbfounded. I think I do know of one person who was prepared for it, though, and even as we speak she'll be ringing up all her friends to tell them so.'

'Not Ellen, surely?'

'No, her sister-in-law, Venetia. I told you about her, didn't I, and the cloak of mystery about her movements this week? Well, just now we were given to understand that Eliza had stepped off the plane this evening and climbed into a taxi to bring her to the studio, with exactly one minute to spare and, somehow or other, it doesn't ring true. It would only have needed the plane to be half an hour late arriving, or some hold up in the Customs for the whole complicated plan to have gone up in smoke. My guess is that she arrived yesterday and has spent the interval recovering from jet lag at Venetia's house in Windsor. Much safer than an hotel, you see, where she might have been recognised, and Venetia has never met any of the rest of the family, so there'd have been no danger of Candida finding out.'

'I expect you're right,' Robin said, as the taxi turned into the hotel courtyard, 'but in any case it's all water under the bridge now.'

'Oh, I know. It's just that I'm so pleased to have that little puzzle cleared up. I do so hate to be baffled, even by something as trivial as that.'

'Then we must just hope that no further bafflements are in store for you here. It will be quite trying enough, as things are, without both of us gawping around in a state of total mystification.'

< 3 >

'How dear of you to come!' Candida said. 'And looking radiant too, I might add. I can't think how you manage it, after what we lot have been through this evening.'

'The very words I was about to say to you.'

This was not strictly true, for I had been watching her, on and off, during the half-hour since our arrival and it

25

had struck me that for once she was looking a little older than her age. This was somewhere in the early forties, a year or two younger than her brother, Benedick, the only son, and more than twice that much older than their sister, Cressida. Cressida had been eleven when Eliza was born, the other two almost grown up and all three had tended to regard her less as a baby sister than as a new puppy, to be petted and scolded by turn; or, as in Candida's case, to be schooled with patience and firmness to come to heel when mistress says so.

'Darling Tessa, always such a comfort! And did you manage to persuade that gorgeous husband of yours to come too?'

'Yes, he's over there, talking to Rodney Blakemore. Wasn't it a stroke of luck running into him the minute we arrived? He's working on a script about a bent copper and the one and only person he has any time for at the moment is a real, live policeman.'

'Oh, what a relief! I was so afraid he'd be bored rigid. Come and meet my naughty little sister. Imagine her turning up like that, literally out of the blue! It's a wonder my poor old Mum didn't have a heart attack.'

'Were you really as stunned as you would have us believe, Candida?'

'Oh, but ab-so-lutely,' she replied, with such passionate sincerity that for the first time it occurred to me that perhaps, after all, she really was a great actress and had known exactly what to expect. However, I dismissed the thought almost immediately because one thing was certain. If so much of a whisper of advance warning had reached her, she would inevitably have taken steps to insure against being so relentlessly upstaged by the naughty little sister.

'It looks as though I'll have to join the queue,' I remarked, drawing her attention to the half-dozen beaming worshippers grouped around Eliza on the other

26

side of the room, 'and I can quite see why. What wouldn't I give to be able to bounce on with all that assurance after about twenty-four hours in an aeroplane?'

'Yes, she's always had enormous reserves of vitality,' Candida conceded in the voice of a doctor giving the case history of a patient, 'but, of course, she's very volatile, you know. There are corresponding reserves of depression to balance things out. She'll most likely be in tears and flat on her back by this time tomorrow.'

'How long does she plan to stay?'

'Two or three days, as far as I've been able to pin her down. Technically speaking, she's still a guest of the studio and they've reserved a room for her here tonight, but I'm trying to persuade her to cancel it and come home with Mother and me.'

'Are you? I should have thought she might have preferred just to flop into bed when this is over, rather than embark on another journey.'

'Then you weren't listening, my darling girl. I've just explained that sooner or later, in a couple of hours, for all anyone can tell, the reaction will set in and she'll touch the depths. When that happens she'll be in far worse trouble in some soul-destroying hotel room than in her own familiar night nursery, with old Nana only two doors away. What could be more cosy and secure, or more exactly what she'll need when this euphoria wears off?'

'Well, you'd know,' I said, not much caring, but thinking that it was a shame about Candida. Despite her well-deserved reputation for bossiness and conceit, she was not, as far as my own knowledge went, an ill-natured woman, or more deceitful than most. Admittedly, she was all too ready to dish out advice, whether invited to or not, but the advice was invariably sound. The trouble was that it was usually delivered in such patronising, headmistressy tones as to infuriate the recipient into takkkkking precisely the opposite course to the one prescribed.

'How are you doing?' Robin asked, when we had found somewhere to rest our plates, glasses and feet.

'Fine, thanks. You?'

'Not so dusty. This lobster isn't half bad.'

'And you had a long talk with Rodney Blakemore?'

'Yes, even managed to make sense of what he was saying. I've invited him round for a drink, if that's all right with you?'

'Oh, sure, but not tomorrow, if possible. I'm supposed to be cheering Ellen up by taking her to the matinée of *Ghosts* and we may have to go round afterwards, so I'm not sure what time I'll be in.'

'No, not tomorrow, the day after. I hadn't forgotten you were going to the theatre, although I wouldn't have described *Ghosts* as a very cheering play.'

'I know, but it does her good to be reminded that other people have sadness in their lives too. Anyway, I'm glad you hit it off with old Rod. You're not given to that kind of instant chumminess, as a rule.'

'Don't be daft, he simply wants me to do some research for him. Nothing confidential, I need hardly say. Just a few facts and figures which I don't carry round in my head to bring out on social occasions. It sounds pretty plodding sort of stuff for what sets out to be a fast-moving thriller, but I suppose he knows best.'

'Oh, that's typical of Rodney, he's a perfectionist. I daresay that by the time it's been through the final editing there won't be any mention of these facts and figures, but his theory is that being so familiar with them himself gives that extra touch of authenticity. I'm glad he's got something going for him again. He's been in the doldrums recently, which is a shame because he's done some good work in his day. What time is he coming, by the way?'

'Six-thirtyish. Rather earlier than I'd have chosen, but he has a dinner date afterwards. I'll try and be back by then, but, if not, I imagine you won't mind holding the fort for a bit? What's going on now?'

'Where?'

'With the nobs,' he said, nodding towards the big table at the top of the room, which had been reserved for the stars and others above the salt. The Deverell family was there in force and the top brass of the television company was also present, along with two or three members of the production crew. The presence of outsiders, plus, no doubt, the fact that, whether by chance or other means, Rosie had been excluded, had brought out the best in her relatives and even Benedick, seated on his mother's left, had only reached the glassy-eyed stage and had evidently managed to restrain himself, so far, from insulting anyone. In a matter of minutes, however, it appeared that all this had changed and a flurry of kinds was taking place, with raised voices all round the table and people bobbing up and down from their seats.

Candida, as usual, was at the centre of the disturbance. She was not a tall woman, a disadvantage she often partially overcame by wearing her pale gold hair piled on top of her head and, although several other people as well were now on their feet, she managed to draw the attention of everyone in the audience to herself. Even Eliza was no competition this time, taking no part in the skirmishing whatever and still seated.

Like everyone else, Robin and I watched in silence as Candida, speaking in tones too low for us to hear, leant across to her mother, who still smiled her dutiful, bright smile, and said a few words to Benedick, who then got up

29

and made a rapid and only slightly unsteady exit from the room.

All this was conducted in a pre-occupied, unself-conscious fashion, as though oblivious of the presence of spectators, an effect which proved to be illusory, however, for her next words were addressed to us.

'Sorry about this slight hitch in the festivities, everyone, but Eliza's feeling rather whacked after that marathon journey of hers and I'm going to take her upstairs, so she can rest for a while before she goes home. In the meantime, do please all carry on with the party. After all, we are here to celebrate my mother's eightieth birthday and, if she's still the same woman as she was at seventy-nine, she won't want any of you to leave before midnight.'

Having delivered these few words, Candida signalled to Harry, the ex-barman, who was Cressida's son and together, each with a hand on her elbow, they escorted Eliza from the room.

She had still been looking bobbish, I thought, when she stood up, but I noticed a spasm of pain, or possibly disgust, twist her mouth as she turned to join her sister and she gripped the back of her chair and clung on to it for a second or two before straightening up.

'I presume there's nothing to stop you and me now fading away into the setting sun?' Robin suggested.

'Well, perhaps not for five minutes,' I said. 'We don't want to look too eager, do you think? Let's finish this champagne, since neither of us is driving and perhaps, with a bit of luck, a few other faders will get in ahead of us. Somehow, whatever Candida may say, I can't see the party getting much fizz back after this episode.'

'The curious part of it was, though,' Robin remarked on the drive home, 'she didn't look ill to me, or even specially tired, but at one point she did seem to be in a certain amount of pain.'

'Oh, blast!' I said, 'I suppose I might have guessed.'

'How could you have guessed?'

'No, I meant there I was, watching everything and everyone like a hawk and feeling so proud of myself for having noticed that little touch, whereas you, whose only thought was how soon we could leave, had seen it as something so obvious as to be hardly worth mentioning.'

'Ah well, that's my training. You'd be the same if you'd spent the past ten or fifteen years dealing with suspects. And you can count yourself lucky that you haven't. It can be a great bore sometimes not being able to smother these reflexes during the carefree social round.'

'Yes, I imagine and, of course, it's not what we both noticed which matters so much as what caused it. For instance, Eliza might have been putting it on. They always said she was the most accomplished actress of the lot.'

'But why would she want to put it on?'

'Well, look at it this way, my dear Watson, it could have been a device for checkmating Candida, who is set on taking her back to the family home tonight. She might have been bored to sobs by the prospect of being tucked up in her own wee beddikins, with dear old Nana popping in to ask whether she remembered to brush her teeth. She might well prefer the anonymous haven of a hotel room, where she could read her book in peace and telephone all her friends. However, useless to try and beat Candida with arguments of that nature, so what to do?'

'Invent a slipped disc, apparently?'

'Quite so, and insist that she'll be as right as rain, providing she can lie perfectly still for twelve hours, but that any movement, such as being jogged around in taxis would knock her out for several days. It's what I would have done, if I'd thought of it in time.'

'In that case, you are bound to have found the answer and I wouldn't dream of arguing. Female duplicity is still a closed book to me.'

'I know and that's partly why I said it. It was a sort of face-saver, really.'

FOUR

< 1 >

Three of the four daily papers which landed on my bed the next morning carried brief reviews of the 'Birthday Tribute' and two of them mentioned Eliza by name, one adding the rider that the London theatre had lost a major star when she escaped from it to another kind of jungle. This gave a certain plausibility to my flights of fancy concerning Eliza's early departure from the party, for I could not imagine many beaming faces round the family breakfast table when these notices were passed back and forth across it.

And that was the last thought I gave to the Deverell family until almost thirty-six hours later, when I went to the front door to let Rodney in.

'Robin's not back yet,' I told him, 'but he won't be long. Come and sit down and have a drink.'

'Rotten news, isn't it?' he asked, casting himself into the armchair opposite mine.

'Rotten,' I agreed, taking it that he referred either to the parlous state of the national economy, or a shake-up at the BBC, both of which had been prominently featured in the news that morning, 'but I daresay it will come all right in the end.'

He stared at me as though I were either raving mad or drunk, which was excusable, since it turned out that he had been talking about the untimely death of Eliza Deverell.

'Good God!' I said, taking a moment or two to recover, 'so she must have been seriously ill, after all.'

'Ill?' he repeated. 'No, I don't think she was ill. Not badly enough to kill her, anyway.'

'How did it happen, then?'

'No one seems to know exactly. The bald facts are that late last night she gave instructions that she was not to be disturbed, and was found dead in her hotel room some time after midday today. The implication being, of course, that she took an overdose.'

'You know, Rodney, I find that very hard to believe.'

'You're not the only one. For my part, I'd stake my life on its being a load of rubbish.'

'When did you hear about it?'

'A few hours ago. It was reported briefly in the early editions and since then the rumours have been flying, as you may imagine.'

'What sort of rumours?'

'Chiefly the one both of us have just ruled out.'

'I'm only going on the brief glimpses I had of her. What makes you so certain it couldn't be true? Do you know something the rest of us don't?'

'There may be others who saw her later and take a different view. All I can say is that she showed no signs of worry or depression when I had a long talk with her the day before the television show.'

'The day before? But, Rodney, what are you talking about? She was still in Australia then.'

'Oh no, she wasn't. She arrived here four days ago.'

'How amazing! Where was she staying? Not with some friends at Windsor, by any chance?'

'Not with friends anywhere. She was incarcerated in a motel near the airport, with books and television and a typewriter for company. She was accustomed to a somewhat restricted and uncomfortable existence in the bush, so she wasn't at all unhappy. Found it pretty plushy, in fact, compared to the mud hut.'

'And that's where you saw her?'

'Yes, over a working lunch, which was served to us in her room. We'd arranged it all in advance. Want to hear?'

'Yes, every word.'

'As I told you, it was a long-standing engagement. I had a letter from her about two months ago, saying she had been invited to take part in what she called a nostalgia spectacular on television, all expenses, including two nights in London afterwards, to be paid by the studio. She told me she was going to grab the offer before they changed their minds because at this precise moment a trip to London was just what she needed, for two reasons. One was for us to meet and have a long talk.'

'Really, Rodney, what a dark horse you are!'

'And what a one-track mind that remark reveals. I can assure you there was nothing of that kind between us. Do you imagine I would be sitting here telling you about it, if there had been?'

'No, I suppose not. Go on!'

'I didn't even rank as a close friend. We first met about fifteen years ago, when I was working as ASM in the theatre. She was always good fun and it was a great feather in the cap of someone in my humble position to be seen around with her. We used to go to movies and art galleries and so forth from time to time, but that's all there was to it, and after a couple of years she got married to this anthropologist bloke and went off to his desert island. I didn't see her again until the year before last when we ran

35

into each other in Sydney, where I was convalescing after picking up some virulent bug in the Far East.'

'Did you ever meet her husband?'

'Only once, just before they married and disappeared into the blue. He seemed all right, attractive, I suppose, in his way. Eliza thought so, anyway and, as far as I know, did till the day of her death.'

'But he didn't come to London this time and I get the impression that he wasn't with her when you met in Sydney?'

'Oh yes, he was. At least, not on that particular day. He'd been despatched to the airport to collect some niece, or cousin, or something, who was coming out to stay with them. Eliza told me that he was giving a series of lectures at the university and they'd rented a house out by the beach for a month or two. We both had a few hours to spare, so we had lunch together and she told me about this project she'd been working on for a six-part original script. She wanted to send me the first one, so that I could let her know what I thought of it. Naturally, I told her I'd be glad to and a few weeks later it arrived on my desk. I hadn't any high hopes of it, to be honest with you. One is always getting trapped into this kind of thing by friends, or friends of friends, and most of them turn out to be utter duds. This was quite different, though, absolutely first rate, in fact. I wrote back at once, telling her so and urging her to get her head down and get it finished.'

'Which she did?'

'Pretty well. Two more episodes turned up a few months later and the standard was just as terrific. In the meantime, I'd started putting out a few feelers at my end and that was all going along nicely too. Everyone I showed the first script to was just as keen to be in on it as I was. Soon after that, though, there was a letter from her saying there was going to be a bit of delay before I got the rest, because she'd hit a

36

snag of some sort. Nothing terribly serious, but she'd need time to work through it and that things would be a whole lot simpler if we weren't separated by several thousand miles and could spend a little time together, chewing it over. Then the next minute I heard about this 'Birthday Tribute' programme, which, as you probably know, was produced by the company I used to be under contract to before I went freelance. So that hurdle was cleared just as easily as all the others had been. It was astonishing how everything fell into place for us all along the line, including all the points we discussed at that last session in her motel room. I suppose, at my age, I should have guessed that it was all turning out to be a damn sight too easy and that sooner or later we'd be up against something really tough, to set us back on our heels. Though, God knows, not even in my most pessimistic moments did I imagine anything on this scale. Well, there it is. I just wanted to make it clear why it would take such a hell of a lot to convince me that Eliza, with everything going for her and the prospect of so much more to come, would have taken her own life.'

I nodded and we were both silent for a moment or two. Then I said, 'I'm sorry Robin's so late. I'm sure he'll be here at any minute, though, otherwise he'd have telephoned.'

These words had the opposite effect from the one I had intended and Rodney stood up. 'Oh, that's all right. I'm not really in a fit state of mind just now to concentrate on that other business, anyway. The only reason for not ringing to suggest postponing it was because anything would have been preferable to hanging around in some pub on my own for an hour and a half. All I needed really was a sympathetic ear and a chance to unburden myself. You've provided both, not to mention a strong drink and I'm really grateful, Tessa. I feel just very slightly better now.'

'I'm glad. Let's keep in touch, shall we? Perhaps, between us and with our separate sources on tap, we can come up with the real explanation for what's happened.'

'OK, I'll ring you in a day or two. We might have lunch.'

For some reason, this remark unloosed a memory and, with my hand on the front door, I said:

'Oh, by the way, there was one other small thing I've been meaning to ask you. You started by saying that Eliza had two good reasons for wanting to come to London.'

'Yes?'

'Well, you've told me one of them, but what was the other?'

'To see a specialist about her back.'

'Her back?'

'Yes, I gather it was her husband, Conrad, who was pushing that idea. Apparently, about two years ago a rope walk she was using to cross a stream collapsed and she fell about twenty feet. No bones broken, but she was badly concussed and she also damaged her spine in some way so they had to get her to a hospital in Australia for treatment. She was there for over a month and that's when she began writing this script, so some good came out of it, but she'd permanently lost her sense of taste and smell and there were various other complications. Also the back trouble was always liable to recur and when that happened the only panacea was complete rest and a stiff course of pain killers. She told me she'd got to the stage of slipping into that routine automatically, as soon as she felt the slightest twinge. It had meant giving up alcohol, but that never bothered her much. She was one of those people who were born two martinis above par, in any case.'

'How did they manage on the island if there was a real emergency?'

'Same way as if you struck a real emergency in a gale force wind in the Outer Hebrides, I imagine. Conrad had set up a small dispensary, with three or four semi-trained native assistants, who cope with day-to-day things like malaria and so forth and he and Eliza had both done a course in first aid. Anything they couldn't handle became simply a question of whether the patient survived long enough to make the trek across land, sea and air to the mainland.'

'And Conrad had heard about some miracle back healer in London?'

'Right. No quackery, or laying on of hands, mind you. Just a straightforward orthopaedic surgeon, who'd made a reputation for himself in this particular field and had started his own clinic. So when the chance came, that was another incentive to jump on a plane to London.'

'How fascinating!'

'Is it? In what way?'

'I'll explain one day. In the meantime, I don't suppose you happen to remember the name of this orthopaedic wizard?'

'Eliza did mention it, but I've forgotten. Something quite ordinary. Not important, is it?'

'Probably not, just a passing thought. Bye, Rodney. Take care and see you soon.'

< 2 >

'Sorry about that,' Robin said, ten minutes later, having arrived home to discover that Rodney had already left, 'I really did mean to be back in time, but there was a conflict of interests.'

'Something unexpected came up which you couldn't get out of?'

'I didn't think you'd want me to get out of it, seeing that it was a few scraps of information concerning the sudden death of Eliza Deverell. I imagine one of your spies has already relayed that news?'

'Yes, the one who was here just now and I might add that he is ready to tell anyone who will listen that, whatever else, it was not suicide.'

'He may well be right. Impossible to say at this stage, but if she did kill herself she chose a funny way to do it. Then, on the other hand— '

'Well, before you get bogged down in an argument with yourself, would you mind telling me what these scraps consisted of?'

'She'd been out to dinner, where or with whom not yet known, and she arrived back at the hotel some time between eleven and midnight. Can't get closer than that, but, anyway, after eleven when the night shift came on, and by eleven the following morning she'd been dead for between ten and twelve hours. There was a bottle of pills on her bedside table, made up from a doctor's prescription in Sydney. The instructions on the label were to take two pills, as required, eight being the limit for one day. Judging by its size, the bottle had originally contained eighty or a hundred, of which twenty-seven remained and have been sent for analysis. The autopsy was due to take place this afternoon.'

'And?'

'That's the lot, so far, but everything indicates that it was an overdose which did the mischief.'

'Assuming that it was a newly opened bottle, would that amount have been fatal?'

'Oh, certainly. Far less would have done it, specially if combined with alcohol.'

'She didn't drink alcohol when she was on pain killers.'

'Maybe not, but she could have done so earlier in the evening. Anyway, all will be revealed by the *post mortem.*'

'Well, it's all dreadfully sad and shocking. I wonder what on earth drove her to do it?'

'So do I.'

'Which reminds me, Robin, why did you call it a funny way to go? I thought retiring to a lonely bedroom and swallowing a handful of pills was the commonest method of all.'

'Yes, so it is, but it doesn't belong here.'

'Why not?'

'Well, for a start, what was the point of making it all so desperately elaborate and expensive? The kind of suicide you had in mind is usually the easiest for most people, but they don't normally travel to the other side of the world to do it in the full blaze of publicity. There must be dozens of ways of killing yourself and setting it up to look like an accident in the kind of place she was living in and surrounded, as they were, by natural hazards of every shape and size.'

'Perhaps she didn't want her husband to spend the rest of his life reproaching himself for having allowed it to happen?'

'She wasn't so careful about her own family's feelings, though, was she? It's almost as though she'd gone out of her way to ensure that they would suffer publicly, as well as in private. And yet I never heard that she felt vindictive towards them, or indeed had cause to.'

'So, on the whole, you take the view that it wasn't straightforward suicide? That someone else had a hand in it?'

'Certainly not. Whatever did I say to give you that idea? If I have an opinion either way, at this stage, I'd go for accidental death and I think the jury will agree with me. They might possibly bring in misadventure, if they happen to be a censorious lot, on the grounds that she'd had a lot to drink and was too squiffy to remember either that she ought not to combine these particular pills with alcohol, or that she'd already taken more than the standard dose when she reached for the bottle again. I don't envisage anything more damaging than that, but it's still going to sound pretty nasty to her mother.'

'Yes, poor old Evadne, not much fun for her. When will the inquest be?'

'Can't tell you. They may leave it till her husband arrives and that could still be some days off. It's a pretty complicated business even getting as far as Perth or Sydney, by all accounts. I'll keep you posted, though, so far as I can.'

FIVE

< 1 >

Early the next morning I telephoned Ellen, who was in
a sunny mood, Jeremy having been restored to her two
days earlier than expected. By an unfortunate coincidence,
which Toby would doubtless have called inevitable in a
man so deficient in tact, his telephone call to announce
this change of plan had interrupted the opening titles of
'Birthday Tribute', and when it was all over Ellen had
been too engrossed in making plans for the resumption
of their domestic bliss to give another thought to the
programme.

'It was a more serious omission than you realised,'
I told her, 'in view of what's happened now. I do so
wish you could at least have seen Eliza as she was that
evening.'

'Me too, and what an appalling thing. So weird too. I
mean, imagine coming all this way and taking part in the
junketings and all the time having this in mind!'

'Yes, that's what a lot of people find hard to swallow.'

'Still, it must be true, don't you think? Even harder to
imagine someone doing a thing like that just out of the
blue. I suppose you have no idea what was behind it?'

'No, although I don't see why that should stop us

having a go at finding out, and here's one thing you could do to start the ball rolling.'

'Something I can do? You must be joking!'

'On your head, as it happens. First of all, what's the name of Venetia's husband?'

'Alec Henderson.'

'Oh, good! That'll do nicely.'

'I'm sure he'll be relieved to hear it.'

'Meaning it's neither so very unusual, nor so very ordinary as to make it easy to remember, which is how it should be for my purpose. What does he specialise in?'

'Orthopaedics.'

'Better still. That just about clinches it. You see, I had an interesting talk with a friend of mine called Rodney, yesterday evening, bits of which I shall now repeat to you.'

When I had done so, I added:

'I wondered at the time why she would need to spend four whole days at a motel. It seemed a disproportionate amount of time to recover from jet lag, but now we have the answer. She wanted to set aside one of them for her business with Rodney and the other for a medical consultation. That's most likely why she stuck herself out near the airport. Equally handy for London and Windsor, you see. No doubt, the studio laid on a car and driver to take her to the clinic and, naturally, her appointment would have been made in her married name, so none of the staff would have realised she was anyone special and it also explains Venetia's contortions. She knew Eliza was going to see her husband, but, not being a complete fool presumably, he hadn't told her which day. All she did know was that no one else must get to hear about it.'

Ellen was silent for so long that I thought we had been cut off, but at last she said:

'Well, you've obviously worked this all out, but I don't understand what difference it makes. Are you suggesting

44

that Alec told Eliza her condition was incurable and bound to deteriorate and that's what made her kill herself?'

'No, I'm not. All I'm suggesting is that when there's a sudden death, suicide or otherwise, it's important to find out whatever you can about the events leading up to it. Mostly, it's quite a simple matter to piece it together from the accounts of people who saw and talked to her during that time, but this case is unique. From the moment she left Sydney until she walked on to the stage four days later her movements were shrouded in secrecy and she lived in a sort of limbo. By sheer fluke, I came across one person who spent a few hours with her, but there may be half a dozen others, each with his own tale to tell. So what I'm saying is that, if Alec Henderson was one of them, he ought to let the coroner or police know about it, because no one is going to come looking for him.'

'OK, Tessa, I'll pass it on. Not that I'd dream of telling him myself. He'd only look down his nose and tell me to mind my own business, but I daresay Venetia knows how to handle him.'

< 2 >

Candida was next on my agenda, having arrived there by a process of elimination. The immediate impulse had been to write some conventional words of sympathy to Evadne, but composing such letters can be a demanding job at the best of times and in this case the circumstances had rendered it beyond my powers. One alternative would have been to follow Lord Melbourne's advice and done nothing and another to put myself on the right foot, when the time came, by sending flowers to the funeral, but this too seemed inappropriate for various reasons, one being that the only words I had addressed to Eliza during her lifetime were 'Oh, hello', just before it ended.

So that only left Candida as a means of communication and I dialled the Kensington number and asked if it would be convenient to speak to her. There followed an interval of several minutes, at the end of which I was told that she was engaged at present, but please to leave my name and number and she would call me back. I complied, although counting the battle already lost, with the result that when she did call me back a few hours later I had already forgotten the words I had intended to use on her.

Fortunately, she was not so handicapped herself and did not wait for explanations:

'Do forgive me, Tessa,' she said in her penitent, little-girl voice, 'you must think me foully rude, but I was closeted with that dreary policeman when you rang up and since then there hasn't been a single minute. I am so sorry.'

'Oh no, it's very sweet of you to bother with me at all, as things are at present,' I said, trying to match her effusiveness, which had effectively made me feel like a blundering busybody. 'Was he really dreary?'

'No, I suppose he was all right in his peculiar way, quite kind really. The trouble was that he would insist on talking to my poor old Mum, despite all my swearing that there was nothing in the world she could add to what I had already told him and you can imagine what a hideous ordeal that was for her, coming on top of everything else?'

'Oh yes, indeed,' I replied in grave tones, also imagining Evadne's frustration and disappointment if she had been denied the hideous ordeal and the chance to put on the noble suffering act to melt the heart of the gruffest police-man. 'As a matter of fact, that's partly why I rang up this morning. I'm going to write to your mother, of course, only this doesn't seem to be quite the moment, so I wanted you to give her my dearest love and also to tell me how she's

46

bearing up and whether there's any tiny thing I could do to help.'

'Darling Tessa, how very sweet of you! She's absolutely shattered, of course, poor old love.'

'Yes, naturally, she would be.'

'As a matter of fact, darling, if you're serious, there is one real act of kindness you could do for both of us.'

'Oh, great!' I said, trying to sound as though I had been serious.

'Now, you must swear on your honour to tell me if it's a nuisance or the slightest bit inconvenient, because I shall understand perfectly, but I have a heavy session with the solicitors coming up tomorrow afternoon and I wondered if you could be an angel and spare a couple of hours to come and sit with her?'

'Well, yes, I suppose so – I mean, I'd be delighted to, if you're sure she'd like it.'

'But of course she would. She adores you, as you know so well, and you have just the right brand of unsoppy sympathy, which is what's needed at the moment. Benedick does his best, but he's far too emotional and it usually ends up with them having a silly row about something completely trivial. Cressy has a matinée tomorrow, so she's no good and it would be really marvellous if you could help us through this crisis.'

'In that case, I'll be glad to. What time do you want me?'

'She usually has a little rest after lunch, so no hurry. If you could make it three thirty, that would do beautifully.'

'OK, Candida, I've got a lunch date on the other side of London, but that shouldn't interfere.'

'And don't break your neck, darling. Ten minutes either way won't matter, and Nana will be around to let you in whatever time you arrive. Thanks, Tessa, you're a true friend.'

47

'Which chatterbox was that?' Robin asked, having come in and poured himself a drink while this conversation was in progress.

'Candida.'

'Oh, really? I hadn't placed her as the garrulous type.'

'She's not, which is what makes it so odd. Normally, she's vague and abstracted, her mind dwelling on higher things, or else speaking in words of one syllable, to make sure I catch the drift, but this business of Eliza seems to have knocked some of the stuffing out of her. She was scraping the bottom of the flattery barrel to find some more to pour over me.'

'To what end, do you suppose?'

'The immediate one was to pin me down to spending a couple of hours with Evadne tomorrow afternoon, while she visits the solicitors, and that's pretty flattering in itself, when you come to think of it. I mean, why me?'

'Didn't she tell you?'

'In a half-hearted sort of way. Something about Cressida having a matinée and Benedick getting on his mother's nerves. All very true, no doubt, but it still doesn't explain why I should be needed. Apart from everything else, they have their old nurse on the premises to minister to her every need.'

'Perhaps she gets on Evadne's nerves too?'

'I shouldn't be surprised, but that still leaves a pretty big choice. She must have dozens of cronies of her own generation who'd leap at the chance of rushing round for a nice, cosy session and picking up all the inner circle gossip.'

'And there, I suspect, you have your answer.'

'How so?'

'It's very likely the thought of her old mother gossiping away to the cronies, who'd be dining out on it for weeks to come, is what inspired Candida to invite you instead.'

'Something on those lines did occur to me, I admit, but, again, why me?'

'By a logical process. Don't you remember telling me the other day how, when you were at Bath, Evadne worked herself up into a great state over her granddaughter setting up house with this unsuitable young man and, having none of her close relatives handy to pour out her troubles to, picked on you?'

'Of course I remember, but this is different.'

'Not so very. The point is that you proved yourself to be a valuable asset in this crisis. You lent a sympathetic ear, not shrugging it off with a few consoling platitudes, with the result that in no time at all Evadne had reverted to her old impervious self. Even more to the point, you never repeated anything she had told you. Your insatiable curiosity, combined with the phobia about betraying a confidence, has stood you in good stead there and is not likely to have gone unremarked by Candida.'

'Well, it would be nice to believe that she had such a high opinion of me, but perhaps I shouldn't let it go to my head. After all, there wasn't anything so electrifying about Evadne's *grande dame* mask slipping for once and revealing the screaming virago lurking underneath. Most people might be reassured to discover that she still had ordinary human feelings, just like the rest of us.'

'Yes, but I don't think it's that sort of indiscretion which Candida is afraid of now. It's more likely that, the cause of Eliza's death having been made known to her, Evadne might lose control and start flinging out a few theories of her own about who might have been involved.'

'But, Robin, how could anyone except Eliza herself have been involved? Death by your own hand surely means exactly what it says?'

'Yes, indeed, but it begins to look as if there is just

49

a possibility that it may not have been as simple as that.'

'Does it, indeed? Why didn't you tell me as soon as you came in?'

'Because you were talking on the telephone.'

'Try not to be too annoying. Just tell me now!'

'I haven't read it, but I've been told that the *post mortem* report revealed that a somewhat larger dose of the pain killer than the prescribed one had been taken not more than four hours before death, in addition to a hefty dose of barbiturates.'

'Well, I never! Would that be enough to kill you?'

'In certain circumstances, without a doubt, Tess. As for instance when combined with alcohol.'

'But Eliza never touched alcohol.'

'She did on this occasion, which I suppose does something to bolster the suicide theory. On the other hand, perhaps she didn't know what she was doing.'

'I find it hard to imagine anyone tossing off a strong drink without realising it.'

'Perhaps I should have said: "Didn't know what was being done to her." '

'Like someone could have mixed barbiturate with the pain killers?'

'It's possible, don't you think? No, I gather you don't, and I must say it is the last reaction I'd have expected from you.'

'Yes, we do seem to have switched roles this time. It's usually me who looks for the sinister explanation, whereas you go for the straightforward, obvious one.'

'So what has happened to change all that?'

'Well, you see, Robin, I can accept the fact that she might have swallowed an alien pill without knowing it. It's the alcohol which bothers me. No one could take a strong dose of whisky or gin by mistake, even blindfolded. The smell alone would give it away at once.'

'Exactly, and didn't Rodney tell you that, as a result of her accident, Eliza had lost her sense of smell?'

'Yes, so he did. I'd forgotten that.'

'As it happens, the sense of smell is lodged somewhere in the brain and is quite unconnected with the taste buds. Even a mild concussion can put it out of action, sometimes permanently, but the odd part is that those so afflicted often become convinced that they have lost the sense of taste as well.'

'But since it's not true?'

'Not true in the medical sense, but nevertheless there'd probably be a delayed reaction, particularly with gin or vodka, which are colourless. Someone might realise within seconds that the glass of clear liquid they had just swallowed was not, after all, plain water, but by then it would be too late to do anything about it.'

'Although I suppose it could have been deliberate this time. I can understand anyone contemplating suicide wanting to provide themselves with a little Dutch courage.'

'I agree, but somehow that wouldn't apply here. I may be wrong, but I'd have thought that cutting out alcohol, in all its forms, would have become too much of a way of life for her to turn to it as a nerve booster. What may be more to the point, I see no reason why she should have needed one. It is hard to believe that anything so catastrophic can have occurred during her three days in London as to drive her to suicide. Therefore, we have to conclude that she had planned it down to the last detail weeks, if not months, ago and that whatever fears she may have had would have been resolved by then. Nor could there have been a question of needing to make sure that the pills on their own would be effective. She had stacks more of them in her luggage, if she'd wanted to double or treble the dose.'

'Which means that, if she was murdered, it was by someone who didn't know that she never touched alcohol?'

51

'Or by someone who wanted it to look that way.'

'Yes, I see what you mean. Who was she dining with that evening, by the way? Does anyone know?'

'No. She left the hotel at about eight. One of the commissionaires remembers that much because she asked him to call her a cab. Unfortunately, she gave her destination to the driver herself and he did not hear it.'

'And is there anything to suggest that someone went up to her room after she came in again?'

'Couldn't tell you, I'm afraid. No doubt, those wheels have started turning and who knows what dust they may throw up, but that's as far as my information goes at present and something tells me there's not likely to be a hell of a lot more to come.'

'Why not?'

'Because I've no doubt that numerous people knew her room number and I see no reason why any of them should bother to deny it. Just picture the scene for yourself. No domestic staff trundling trolleys up and down at that time of night. Just a small trickle of guests going back and forth from their rooms to the lifts, all intent on their own affairs, most of them strangers in this country and none probably staying more than one or two nights. What chance do you imagine there would have been for so much as one of them noticing a single individual emerging from a particular room? Or that, having done so, he would make a note of the time and still be around to provide the information when it was needed?'

'On the other hand, if he were and if the single individual happened to be a celebrity of some sort, I suppose it could have made enough impression on him to stick in his mind?'

'Like a well-known actor or actress, you mean?'

'That would be an obvious example.'

'Not a terribly good one, though, in my opinion. If it had

been you, for instance, I am sure you would have taken the elementary precaution of adopting a little, light disguise. I am not referring to black wigs and false moustaches. Just a headscarf and a stoopy walk would have been enough to throw most observers off the scent.'

'So, in other words, if there was a murderer on the loose that evening, there's a fat chance of finding out who it was?'

'Oh, I didn't say that. I only mean that it won't be just a simple matter of finding out who was the last known person to have seen her alive and starting from there. There'll be a hell of a lot to dig out about the victim herself, for one thing.'

'Yes, I see what you mean.'

'Not that it concerns me officially,' he added. 'It's just that circumstances having conspired for me to be in at the death, so to speak, I am rather enjoying the role of informed outsider.'

'That's good,' I told him. 'We shall be in the same boat for once and it will inspire me to strain every nerve to keep pace with you.'

SIX

< 1 >

Rodney had explained to me, without much in the way of apology on his side or surprise on mine, that the venue for our lunch date, which was a pub on the fringes of Covent Garden, had been chosen less for its food and ambience than its clientèle.

'Not exactly yer café society lot. Rather low level, in fact, but they're a type which figured prominently in my life until recently and I've come to feel at home with them.'

'That's nice,' I said.

'No need to be snooty. The grub's not all that bad.'

'Well, just so long as it's not too crowded, Rodney. I sometimes get bored with the conversation of the people at the next table.'

'No danger of that, dear. This lot are more inclined to communicate by grunts and nudges.'

The odd thing was that after this somewhat daunting introduction, they turned out to look exactly like all the other people who were crowding into similar pubs and wine bars in that part of London and, had I not known better, I might have taken them for tourists who were there because they didn't know any better, or small-time office workers who had no choice.

We had lunch upstairs in a room just large enough to hold eight tables and slightly more up market in style than the saloon bar and here there were even one or two gangs of lady crooks among the lunchers, although cleverly disguised as housewives who had just spent a merry morning going round Marks & Spencer.

However, it was beginning to dawn on me by then that neither the place nor its clients had any more sinister associations than were to be found anywhere else in London, including the Ritz, but had most likely been chosen simply because it was cheap.

At this point in my private deliberations I began chiding myself for having failed to guess that Rodney was on his beam ends and too proud to admit it. If I'd had the wit to grasp it earlier I could have invited him to lunch at Beacon Square, which would have solved his problem and saved me the necessity of choosing between shepherd's pie and lasagne, both of which, judging by the heaped-up plates which had just been flung down for the female crooks with the green plastic bags, looked equally unappetising.

So, one way and another, our meeting had not got off to a bright start and I tried to make amends for this by professing a great interest in his current work on the police story, although with little success there either.

In my experience, television writers do not normally need much encouragement to hold forth about their work, except, presumably, in the presence of other television writers who may be on the look-out for ideas and not too particular where they take them from, but Rodney seemed positively uninterested and finally admitted as much. My suggestion of fixing a new date for him to talk it over with Robin was greeted without enthusiasm, and when I pretended not to notice this and brought out my diary, he said:

'It's kind of you, Tess, but I honestly don't feel there'd be much point at the moment.'

'OK, whatever you say.'

'Now don't get huffy, for God's sake. It's not that I'm ungrateful. On the contrary, I'd like to meet Robin again sometime, we got on pretty well, but I don't want to sail under false colours.'

'Why should you— Oh, you don't mean the project has been shelved?'

'Not exactly. The main trouble is that I can't seem to get to grips with it just now. The interest has gone. I thought coming back here today might revive it, but it hasn't worked. I'm not seriously worried because it's probably just a question of time. Hope so, anyway.'

'Is this what they call writer's block?'

'No, that's when you're struggling to write something, anything, and the words won't come. It's like sitting down in front of a brick wall and trying to force your way through with a teaspoon. There's no brick wall this time; the other way round, in fact.'

'I'm afraid you've lost me now, Rodney.'

'Yes, I'm sorry. You must get the impression I'm going bonkers, or something, but the fact is – you remember my telling you about that script of Eliza's?'

'Yes, of course. You were very impressed.'

'Not half as much as I am now. After that morning we spent together she must have worked all through the rest of the day and most of the night and next day too, I shouldn't wonder. She'd completed the last episode and re-written parts of the two preceding ones to tie in with it and it's a smasher, I have to tell you. There's a bit of tidying up still to be done, but you could show it to anyone exactly as it is and I can't see any reason why they'd want to lose a minute getting their hands on it.'

'You mean she sent it to you before she died?'

'That's exactly what I mean. It arrived by special messenger that morning, but the hellish part is that I wasn't able to get started on reading it till the evening, so I missed my chance to tell her how terrific I thought it was. I feel bad about that. Like I'd let her down.'

'Bad enough to neglect your own work, as a result?'

'I feel it is my own work. I was in on it from the start and I want to see it through to the end. She'd never have got to the point she did without my help and encouragement and I owe it to her now to put everything else aside. No need to look at me like that, Tessa. I'm not being sentimental about it and it's not just Eliza's memory that motivates me. On the contrary, I wouldn't waste ten minutes over these scripts if I didn't think them so damn bloody good.'

'OK, you're the expert, so I'll take your word for it, but why should it be necessary to neglect your other work when you also tell me that anyone would take this thing of Eliza's just as it stands?'

'And so they would, but that won't do for me. I want it to be absolutely right, absolutely as it would have been, if we'd had the chance to work on it together for a few more weeks. Don't worry, it won't take for ever. A couple of months, less maybe, and then I can bow out.'

'How about credits?'

'What credits?'

'Will this go out as a joint effort, or your own script, based on an idea by Eliza, or what?'

'Haven't given it a thought yet. Depends, really. As it stands now, it's eighty per cent her own work, but, naturally, if whoever takes charge of it should want any major changes or additional dialogue, I shall have it in the contract that I'll be the one to do it. In that case, it might end up as a collaboration. Too early to say, at this stage.'

'I'd have thought it might be a bit more complicated than that.'

'In what way?'

'I was wondering about copyright and so on. Won't her heirs and executors want some say, if not share, in it?'

'Don't see why. Have to get the legal department to check it out before I can be certain, but I have an idea those rules won't apply. Eliza handed the whole bundle over to me before she died, to do what I liked with and no strings. I have her letter to prove it, if anyone raises objections and, so far as I can see, it's just as much my property as the lucky charm she gave me for my birthday eight years ago.'

'And did that bring you luck?' I asked.

'In a way. I'm still here, I've known Eliza and I'm still getting paid for the only work I enjoy and understand. That can't be all bad. Could you do with another glass of wine?'

'I could, but I won't. I have an appointment at half-past three and it would take more than a lucky charm to ward off the evil eye if I were to fall asleep when I get there.'

< 2 >

'Hello, dear,' Nana said, flinging the door wide, after much clanging of locks and pulling of bolts from within, 'come along in. We haven't seen you for ages.'

This was her invariable greeting and designed to conceal the fact that, although she had been expecting me, or someone similar, she had forgotten my name; and ages, in this context, could just as easily have meant four hours as four months.

She was a skittish old party, now in her mid eighties, very jealous of her own and her employers' standing in the world and with a strength in wind and limb which amply made up for what the head lacked.

This was not surprising, for she still enjoyed the good, plain nursery food, which was served to her three times a day by troupes of part-time minions, revelled in theatrical gossip, got her fresh air and exercise by daily excursions to supervise the visiting gardener and was perfectly content to spend the remainder of her waking hours knitting bedjackets for all the family, talking about the old days to anyone who would consent or pretend to listen, and watching soap operas on television.

'Come along through to the drawing room, dear. Her ladyship's still upstairs, but it's getting near her time to come down, so I'll go and call her in a minute. Feel like a cup of tea? I was just going to ring for Maria to bring me a pot.'

'Thank you, Nana, I'd love some in a minute. No hurry, though.'

'Sit down, then and make yourself comfy. Terrible about Eliza, isn't it?' she added, almost as an afterthought.

'Simply appalling. How's Lady Deverell taking it?'

'Beside herself, poor dear. In a great taking, you may be sure. "I'm never going to get over it, Nana," she says, "not if I live to be a hundred." "And nor you will," I tell her, "not if you were to live twice as long." '

'It must have been a fearful shock for you too,' I suggested, not really meaning it, but suspecting both from earlier reactions and the matter-of-fact way in which this moving dialogue had been repeated that her mind had now reached that comfortable stage of senility when a dropped stitch was no less tragic than an old friend dropping off the Eiffel Tower.

She confirmed this by saying, more in resignation than in sorrow, 'Oh, it's been terrible. Never shall I forget the day when they broke it to me. Wednesday, it must have been, or was that the day when they had the show on television? And imagine her turning up like that for it! She always was a harum scarum, even as a child. No end to the pranks she could think up. "You mark my words," I used to tell her, "it'll end in tears one day, if you keep on like this," but she never took a blind bit of notice, just went her own way and finished up getting so tired that she couldn't even remember how many pills she'd taken.'

'What's that you're knitting?' I asked, resigning myself to the fact that no new light was to be cast here on Eliza's death. 'A hot water bottle cover?'

'Oh no, dear, I gave up making them years ago. You are behind the times. We all have electric blankets on our beds these days. Not that Candida approves. Always reminding me not to leave it switched on when I go to sleep. As though I would! No, this is just a little jacket for Rosie's boy. Matinée jackets they used to be called, but Candida says the word's gone out of fashion now. He's called Ned, would you believe? Not Edward or Edmund, just plain Ned.'

'Will he wear it? My cousin, who knows them slightly, says the baby is always dressed in boiler suits.'

'So he is, but I expect that's only because Rosie can't afford any decent clothes for him. Poor girl, I know I shouldn't say this, but you can't help liking Rosie and I feel sorry for her sometimes. We know she's not all she should be, but she does her best for the child and he's a lovely boy, that Ned. They say he screams all the time, but I had charge of him for three or four hours the other evening and he was good as gold.'

'Did you, Nana? Which evening was that?'

'Oh, some time this week. Can't remember days any more. Rosie didn't give me any warning, though, that I do remember. Just dropped in when they were all out somewhere. I was thinking it must be getting on time to

60

switch on the television for the snooker when the doorbell rang and there she was. Some tale about an appointment she had to go to where she couldn't take the baby with her and would I mind looking after him for an hour or two because that friend of hers she lives with had got the flu. Very smart and well turned out she looked, too. Wouldn't have recognised her if I hadn't had my glasses on. Hair all smarmed down and high-heeled shoes and I don't know what all. "You should have gone on the stage, just like all the rest of them," I told her,' Nana added in a resentful tone, evidently unable to envisage any other career for a smart looking girl and probably including herself among the élite by virtue of having joined the ranks during the run of *Peter Pan*.

'How long was she gone?'

'That you may well ask. I was a bit cross with her, as it happens, because she was away a good deal longer than she'd said. Not that I minded for myself, but I was afraid the poor little chap would wake up and start feeling hungry. It was all right, though. I gave him some of that rosehip I always keep by me and he was good as gold.'

'I wonder where she was going that she couldn't take him with her. She doesn't usually let it bother her.'

'That's what I thought myself, seeing how only a night or two before she'd dragged the poor mite off to the television studio, but it must have been something special, judging by the way she'd got herself up for it. Ah, here we are, then!' she added putting her knitting down and easing herself out of the armchair as the door opened. 'And how are you feeling now, dear?'

'A little rested, thank you, Nana. I believe, I really believe, I managed to close my eyes for ten minutes. And here's my dear little Tessa come to cheer me up. Isn't that sweet of her? Could you see about some tea, please, Nana?'

61

'What are you going to have with it? Scones and butter? Some of that chocolate cake you like?'

'Whatever you think, darling. I'm sure I couldn't eat anything myself, but I know Tessa has a hearty appetite. And it must be nearly time for your Australian programme, isn't it? I expect you'd rather have yours upstairs.'

There followed a small battle of wills, in which Nana, not having heard the last question, or pretending she had not, set off to the kitchen, leaving her knitting on the chair, as Evadne noticed a fraction too late to recall her.

'I'll take it, shall I?' I asked, gathering up the wool and needles.

'Oh, how very kind and thoughtful of you, darling. Poor old Nana, she's getting so vague,' Evadne continued when I returned from my errand, 'I often wonder how we'd ever manage without her and one wouldn't want to hurt her feelings, but there are times, which I wouldn't admit to anyone else outside the family, when she does get the tiniest bit on my nerves.'

Having heard her make the same admission a dozen or more times to anyone within earshot, I waited for her to continue.

It is a mistake, however, to assume that anyone, even those like Evadne who spend much of their day living out a script of their own creation, can ever be entirely predictable and her next confession, which came a few minutes later, more than made up for the banality of the first one.

Still pursuing the subject of what a sweet old drag Nana was, she burbled on for a bit about how in times of stress and deep sorrow one so longed to be utterly alone sometimes, or able to talk confidentially with old and trusted friends, adding that in the current crisis of her life I was the true and trusted one who fulfilled this need to perfection. Even this I swallowed with only one small, self-deprecating headshake and found myself being promptly put in my place:

'No, of course you think that's just eyewash. No reason why not. You have never been through any experience remotely like this, I pray God you never have to, and you didn't even know our darling Eliza.'

'I think I can understand something of what you must be feeling,' I said, not best pleased to have my inadequacies pointed out.

'Yes, yes, of course,' Evadne said, patting my hand, 'but the real point is, my dearest girl, that you may be in a unique position to help me in a practical way, which would be more valuable than all the sympathy in the world.'

'Oh well, in that case, if you really think so, Evadne, I'll certainly— '

'Candida has been telling me about your husband. Apparently, she was talking to him at that macabre party. Not that it was macabre at the time. I wouldn't be so ungrateful as to say that when everyone had gone to so much trouble, but looking back on it now, after what's happened, I can hardly bear— Do forgive me,' she said, pausing here for a little eye dabbing. 'Where was I?'

'Candida had been talking to Robin.'

'Yes, and I must say you've kept it very dark, Tessa. I knew he was in the police, naturally, but Candida tells me he's something fearfully important in the CID, and don't attempt to deny it because we all know that she can be relied upon to get her facts right.'

'Even if she were, I don't see what help it could be to you.'

'Then I shall let you into a little secret, knowing full well that it won't go any further. We had two police officers here yesterday. Not in Robin's class, I must explain, but very

63

pleasant and well spoken and tumbling over themselves with apologies for intruding on us.'

'Oh, good!'

'So far as it went but, for all their honeyed words, I had the strong impression that they haven't finished with us yet and will be back sooner or later with more questions, which may not be so easy to answer. It seems a little hard that we should be subjected to this sort of thing, on top of losing our darling girl, but I suppose it would be useless to complain.'

'Yes, I'm afraid so, but what gave you the idea that they meant to come back with questions you'd find hard to answer?'

'Because we feel instinctively, and this is where I speak in utmost confidence, that they are not convinced that my poor baby's death was due to some horrible, tragic mistake. They are simply not capable of taking in such a concept. At any rate, not until they have worn us out in their search for some other explanation, perhaps more in line with their experience, given the sort of people they normally have to deal with.'

'So what is it you want Robin to do? He would have no power to interfere, you know.'

'Oh, of course I realise that. Such an idea never entered my head. It is simply that I should be so very grateful, my dearest, and so long as it wouldn't be breaking any rules, if he could find out what sort of alternative they are likely to have in mind and the kind of things they will want to know.'

This request revealed such a profoundly unrealistic view of the situation that I was quite at a loss to answer and sat for some moments in silence, hoping thereby to create the impression that I was giving serious thought to the matter which, in a sense, I was, although not quite on the lines she can have intended. My aim, in short, was to maintain the delicate balance between disabusing her of her fantasies, while at the same time finding out what lay behind them.

Finally I said, 'I can ask him, of course, if you wish me to, but I think I can tell you here and now what his answer would be. It would take the form of another question and he would want to know what it is that you're afraid of.'

It was Evadne's turn to become silent and thoughtful while, as I could tell from her blank expression, various ways of playing the hand presented themselves. Not unexpectedly, she settled for the most dramatic.

'I suppose', she announced in tones of quiet simplicity, 'that what I'm most afraid of is the truth.'

'Oh, really? Oh, I see! Well, I imagine in that case, Evadne, Robin's advice, if the police were to question you again, would be to insist on having your solicitor present.'

The comical side of this remark did not strike me until I had uttered it and, just in case Evadne had caught it too, I galloped straight on: 'Naturally, I realise that in the normal way you would hardly need protection from the truth, but I assume it's not yourself you are trying to protect, but someone else and that you're afraid that you might inadvertently come out with something that could incriminate them?'

'Incriminate? No, that is much too strong a word. For all I know, it may be a breach of the law to take your own life, but I wouldn't regard anyone who did so as a criminal, would you?'

'So you do believe Eliza committed suicide?'

'I also believe that she had made up her mind to do so from the moment she decided to come to London.'

'And I am sure you must have your reasons, but the odd thing is that someone who knew her quite well takes her coming almost as proof enough that she intended no such thing. Why spend all that time, trouble and money, when the opportunities for doing it out there on the island were all around her?'

'Then perhaps this person, whoever it may be, did not know her quite well enough to guess that she might wish to spend her last days on earth surrounded by her own family and also to make sure that when the time came they would understand and not blame her for what she had done.'

The conversation had taken such an unexpected turn and was moving along at such a clip that I was finding it hard to keep up, as well as conscious of being sadly under-rehearsed. Wading out of the morass and with the air of one giving weighty consideration to the subject, I said:

'Well, they have to take every eventuality into account and then try to get to the truth by a process of elimination and, presumably, suicide would figure high on the list. On the other hand—'

'Yes?'

'It's not really for the police to make up their minds one way or the other. The first thing is to line up all the medical and other evidence for the coroner's court and after that it's for them to decide on the cause of death. I imagine you or someone in the family might be called on to describe her state of mind immediately beforehand, but I doubt if the verdict would be much influenced by your answers. So perhaps you are worrying unnecessarily.'

We were interrupted at this point by the arrival of the tea tray and, after thanking Maria for her goodness in bringing it and showering her with compliments about how beautifully it was set out, Evadne made a great performance of consulting my every wish in the matter of milk and sugar, scones with or without raspberry jam, or whether I would prefer cucumber sandwiches to start with. I had

66

the impression, though, that this was a purely mechanical exercise and that beneath the flow of chat her mind was humming away like a beleaguered bee. So I allowed her to play it out to the end and, having done so, she said:

'Well, that is some comfort, I suppose. It is certainly a relief to know that I should not be forced to speak of my poor darling's sufferings during her last days. Days? What am I talking about? Months would be more like it, probably even years.'

'Was it her illness which caused her such – distress?'

'Illness? Oh, you mean her poor back? Yes, that was a trial too, but I don't believe it troubled her nearly so much as she would have had us believe. I doubt if you can understand this, but I always felt it was a way of expressing her grief over losing the baby, which went too deep for her to talk about openly.'

'I never knew she had a baby. Did it die?'

'It was stillborn, you see. A little boy, too, which she'd been so longing for. It was all due to this terrible fall she had when she was seven months pregnant. What she was doing, capering about like that in her condition is something I shall never understand, but of course I blame Conrad just as much for that as for the rest of the sorry tale. If only he'd taken proper steps to get her into hospital earlier, I daresay it would all have turned out differently, but he was too mean and callous, that was the trouble.'

'Though, to be fair, I suppose it must have been difficult for him, seeing how cut off from civilisation they were?'

'And whose fault was that, I should like you to tell me? Besides, I feel sure he could have moved mountains, if he'd wished to, but obviously he didn't and it was the same story, when they told her after it was all over, that she could never have another child. Nothing will ever convince me that something couldn't have been done about it, if only he'd been willing to spend the money to bring her over to see a specialist in London.'

'But it can't have been just meanness, surely? Wouldn't the family have chipped in for that kind of emergency?'

'Yes, and naturally we offered to and were told to mind our own business. Not in those words, of course. Eliza put it very tactfully in her letter turning down the offer, only just stopping short of claiming that the decision was all her own. But you are right, as usual, Tessa. I don't believe it was just meanness, pure and simple, although he is almost pathological in that respect. I am certain in my own mind that things suited him very well just the way they were.'

'Meaning that he never particularly wanted to have children?'

'Yes, I am afraid that is exactly what I mean.'

'Well, I can see that it would have created complications for him. Not many people would have relished the idea of bringing up a child in those primitive surroundings. I suppose he realised it would oblige him to leave his beloved island and move back to dreary old civilisation, at least for a year or two.'

'Perhaps he did and perhaps not. What is more likely, to my mind, is that he would never have contemplated leaving and would have over-ridden whatever objections Eliza might have had to staying on. But that still wouldn't have satisfied him and the plain truth is that the baby would have provided another outlet for some of Eliza's love and attention. And there was the rub, you see. He wanted her entirely to himself. It would have suited him to perfection to have this potential rival disposed of, with no possibility of any more to follow.'

'Honestly, Evadne, I feel quite giddy. You make him sound like a monster in human form.'

'I am sorry if you find it shocking and distasteful, but,

with my hand on my heart, that is precisely what I believe him to be.'

'Well, all I can hope is that, to some extent at least, they were of the same mind about it. If the baby was an accident, not planned or much wanted by either of them, she wouldn't have felt so bad about losing it and, I've always heard that she positively enjoyed that primitive life on the island and she was devoted to her husband.'

'All very true in the early days, when it was such a great adventure, but that was ten years ago, you know and she was hardly more than a child. He was an attractive, good-looking man, in his way, quite a lot older than her, with a strong personality and reputed to have a brilliant mind. She was dazzled by him, but even in those days she had never expected to live out the great adventure for the rest of her active life. The understanding was that they would spend two or three years on the island, while he buried himself among this silly tribe and collected all his notes and tapes and so on. After that he'd settle down at some university and Eliza would have a permanent home in England. It was understood that it might have been necessary to return to the island for brief spells every so often, to keep his work up to date, but there was never any suggestion that she would accompany him.'

'So why did everything change, I wonder? Was it the tribe or was it Eliza that became the obsession?'

'A bit of both, in my opinion. He's a peculiar man, as you must have realised by now. Far more peculiar than anyone of us was prepared for.'

'Including Eliza?'

'Oh, undoubtedly. Her life out there has been very troubled and difficult.'

'To the extent where she might have reached the point where suicide seemed to be the only way out?'

'I really couldn't tell you, my darling, but I do think

a case could be made out for believing so. She had made several attempts to leave him, you know, but he always got round her in the end.'

'And you absolutely rule out the idea that it could have been an accident?'

'No, I don't, not at all. That would certainly be the most satisfactory – realistic explanation, but unfortunately – poor old Nana is such a chatterbox, you know. It makes things rather difficult.'

'Does it? How?'

'Well, it was a sort of family joke, you see and it cropped up again when Eliza was here this time. She was so well known for her scattiness and so well aware of it herself that she made an absolute rule, whenever she was on any kind of pills or medicine, of putting out the full dose for each day as soon as she got up in the morning and then, when she went to bed that night, she'd take whatever happened to be left over all in one go. It was her little dodge for making certain of not taking too many by mistake.'

'Yes, I see. And you don't genuinely believe it was suicide either, do you?'

'In my heart of hearts, no, perhaps not, but I'd settle for that gladly, if it's the best we can expect. The only alternative that I can see is too shattering and distasteful to contemplate. I don't see how any of us could bear it.'

I was so baffled as to what this alternative could be that I found nothing whatever to say and, taking advantage of the silence, she began to speak very quietly and with great intensity:

'You see, my dear, Conrad, like a lot of brilliant people I have come across in my time, is also a little mad. Furthermore, I consider his behaviour in recent years indicates that he is getting madder by the minute. I believe him to be now totally at the mercy of this obsession of his. That is why I have to be so very careful not to let a word slip out which might put the police on the right track.'

I was beginning at last to get the seeds of an idea of what she was leading up to, but thought it best to wait for her to spell it out for me, which she obligingly did:

'I am not saying he is guilty and I pray God it may never become necessary to establish whether he is or not. All I do say is that he would have been fully alive to the risk of Eliza never returning to the island, or at any rate not for many months, once she had her feet on English soil again, and of forming the resolve that if he could not have her entirely to himself no one else should have her at all.'

SEVEN

< 1 >

'And that was her final word on the subject,' I told Robin, when reporting on the day's events. 'Quite right, too. Silly to spoil a good curtain line with embroidery. Besides, her meaning was perfectly clear.'

'Meaning that before Eliza left the island Mr Hyde spent an hour or two in Dr Jekyll's dispensary concocting some fatal pills to scatter among the genuine ones?'

'That is what I took to be the implication, yes.'

'And the reason why she was so afraid of letting it out to anyone but yourself was because of the scandal that would ensue and the damage it would do to the family image?'

'My interpretation precisely.'

'But why you, I wonder?'

'I suppose because she felt this burning need to tell someone and she knew her secret would be safe with me. What other reason could there be?'

'I can think of two, both rather less flattering than yours. The first is that she needed to rehearse the story in case she had to use it on a less sympathetic audience on some future occasion. Alternatively, and you may like this even less, you were being used as a stand in for that policeman she is expecting to receive another call from and for whose

72

benefit she has every intention of flying this kite. In which case, I consider she was wasting her time.'

'But, if I found it just credible, why shouldn't he?'

'Because, unlike you, he would have no artistic scruples about curtain lines. In fact, far from leaving it there, he would want to get his hands on all the embroidery that was going. For instance, how did Conrad know so far in advance that his wife would need her pain killers during the short time she was to spend in England? She could hardly have been in trouble with her back when she left, otherwise she'd have been in no fit state to make the journey.'

'Perhaps he simply gambled on the fact that the rigours of the journey would be enough in themselves to bring on an attack?'

'In that case, he was mistaken, wasn't he? Your friend, Rodney, who saw her soon after she arrived, reported that she was in excellent health and spirits.'

'But, Robin, the point is, surely, that, since it was a recurring trouble, she would either return to the island within the week, or else would stay on here and, sooner or later, inevitably have recourse to the pills. QED.'

'QE nothing of the kind. According to Eliza's own words, the secondary, if not main reason for agreeing to take part in the television show was to see an orthopaedic surgeon and this, as is now known, is exactly what she did. What more likely, once he had studied the X-rays and made various tests, than that he would have taken her off whatever pills she was on then and prescribed a new lot? All specialists do that, as a matter of course, after the first consultation. Otherwise the patient wouldn't feel he was getting his money's worth. Conrad would have realised this as well as anyone and that his carefully laid plans would depend on her taking some of the original pills within days of her arrival. And then there's another thing.'

'I'm not sure I'm ready for any more.'

'Brace yourself because, even if things had gone his way in that respect, he can hardly have arranged for some accomplice to turn up at the right moment and clinch matters by arranging for Eliza to swallow half a tumbler of neat spirits to help the medicine go down.'

'And the pills wouldn't have been fatal without it?'

'Well, it certainly didn't increase her chances of survival. Of course, we don't know if the old lady genuinely believed all that fandango about her son-in-law committing murder by remote control, or whether she was simply trying it out on you in order to gauge her chances of getting away with it in a higher court.'

'Though not to much purpose, in your view?'

'I wouldn't have thought so. I don't see how anyone could escape the conclusion that, if it was murder, then whoever doctored the pills also substituted neat alcohol for water and furthermore was in the room with her when she drank it. It also occurs to me that Evadne is equally aware of this herself and that therefore the immediate family will be among the prime suspects.'

'Hence the fiction of Conrad being a psychopath, to divert attention from her nearest and dearest? Well, I wouldn't put it past her.'

'I'm glad to hear it because she certainly led you up the garden path in one aspect of the situation.'

'Which one?'

'Eliza was six to eight weeks pregnant when she died.'

'No! Why didn't you tell me that yesterday?'

'Because I didn't see the full report until today and my informant hadn't thought to mention it. So the next question is: was Evadne fooling you over that, too, or had she been fooled by Eliza?'

This conversation took place on the drive down to Roakes Common, where Toby's agent, Jack Pullborough, was

74

spending the night on his way back to London after the opening of some pre-London tour in the north of England.

Toby, although he does not admit it, is rather intimidated by Jack, who is an arrogant snob, with a chip on each shoulder. They have been formed there partly through his own lack of success, both as actor and playwright, each of which at different times had been his own chosen profession, and partly through the poorly concealed belief of there being something socially as well as artistically second rate about agents. As a result of this he tends to dislike all his clients, either for being more talented or better bred than himself, or, in rare cases, both.

His revenge has taken the form of instilling them with the belief that, but for his efforts, they would be on the scrap heap and, furthermore, given the rapidly changing public taste, this was very likely to happen, anyway.

None of this makes him very congenial company and Robin and I had seriously considered declining the invitation to join them for dinner, before putting Satan behind us. This came under the heading of taking the rough with the smooth, for we could not deny that we were only too ready to avail ourselves of Toby's hospitality and Mrs Parkes's cooking at such times as Jack Pullborough was not also doing so.

There were two cars parked near the house on the edge of the Common, both equally eye catching and providing a nice contrast in contemporary life styles. One was a maroon Jaguar, so gleaming and spotless as to give the impression of having been delivered from the dealers that very afternoon, the other an elderly Ford, presenting a ceramic effect of faded blue and brown. The blue was the remains of the original paint and the brown the patches of rust which had encroached on it over the years.

'Who's here, apart from Jack?' I asked Toby, who, with

most untypical civility, had come as far as the front door to greet us.

'I was upstairs and saw your car,' he explained, 'and very glad I was. Let us take a turn round the garden while I tell you what has befallen.'

'Won't your guests find it rather eccentric?' I suggested, as we strolled towards the kitchen garden, in full view of the house.

'They are not exactly my guests,' he replied, 'and I don't care how they find it.'

'Besides,' Robin said, 'I daresay a dash of eccentricity is what they have come to expect. Your gooseberries seem to be doing well this year.'

'Yes, they are. I will bring you some when I come to London tomorrow.'

'How kind! Not a special journey, I trust?'

'No, I rather thought of spending the night, possibly two, if you have no objection.'

It usually takes a Machiavellian combination of sticks and carrots to persuade him to spend so much as a single night in London and only one explanation occurred to me:

'Can this mean that Jack is threatening to spend an extra night here?'

'It is worse than that. Not content with upsetting my life by descending on me himself, he is now doing all in his power to make it even more intolerable by setting that ghastly Rosie loose on the premises.'

'Rosie Deverell? But why should he want to do that?'

'She may have been his main object in coming, for all I know. He is dazzled by the Deverell family, who are not only gloriously celebrated and successful, but gloriously upper class as well. He would use any lever to hoist himself into their good graces and the one he has chosen is to discover in Rosie the promise of becoming one of the foremost dramatists of her generation. He is bent on signing her up before anyone else gets in ahead of him and I am just a pawn on his tatty old chessboard.'

'Very tiresome for you,' Robin agreed, 'but it is only for one evening, presumably? Delighted as we shall be to have your company in London, I can't see any need for you to remain in hiding once the board has been put away and the players departed. Rosie is not likely to bother you again.'

'That is where you underestimate her. According to Mrs Parkes, who was thoughtful enough to bring me a whisky and soda in my room, she also turns out to be one of the foremost scroungers of her generation. Having arrived here this evening and taken one look at the swimming pool, she went into action.'

'She disapproved?'

'On the contrary, it was the very thing she had been searching for. Living in this dump was OK, but one big snag was being so far from the sea. How lovely to know that the next best thing was so near at hand. Mrs Parkes actually heard her say to Jack that she felt sure the pool was hardly used during the week and her lot wouldn't be any bother to anyone because they'd bring their own sandwiches. Imagine my feelings!'

'Yes, that's really rough,' Robin admitted, 'sort of alfresco squatters, you might say. If something drastic isn't done you look like being an exile from your own dear home for the rest of the summer.'

'Oh, I am not beaten yet and my counter attack goes into action tomorrow morning. I shall warn Parkes that there will be a young couple, with even younger child, marauding about in the garden while I'm away and Mrs Parkes will have instructions to provide them with plenty of Coca Cola, or whatever she considers appropriate. That should do the trick. They will welcome the invasion even less than I do and deal with it a lot more ruthlessly if I am not here to cramp their style. We had better go inside now. I just wanted to fill in the background for you.'

It took less than two minutes to discover that Toby had seriously underestimated the opposition.

One of his limitations is the inability to see any good in young women who do not conform to his standards of beauty and elegance. Plain looks, grubby nails and unkempt, shabby clothes are anathema to him and it must be said that Rosie was one of the worst offenders ever to cross his threshold. Her hair looked like the work of some feckless heron who had lost heart when half-way through building a nest out of straw and her apparel for this fine summer evening consisted of dingy, calf-length dress, shapeless, knee-length cardigan and muddy brown boots. By ignoring her existence, so far as was physically possible, he had failed to recognise a quality she possessed which would have been instantly perceptible to anyone else, with the exception of a short-sighted deaf mute.

Like her Aunt Eliza, Rosie had charm. She did not flaunt it in any way, speaking only in brief, sometimes disconnected sentences, but it seemed to emanate from her in an almost tangible way, just as I had noticed in Eliza while watching her from another side of the room. There were other resemblances too. Like Eliza, she was a rebel, who had no truck with half measures. Having side-stepped all the values and traditions she had been brought up to admire, she had gone to the furthest extreme. A good many girls of her generation had left the safety and comfort of their homes to wander off like gypsies and lead untidy lives in squalid surroundings, but few of them can have created such a trail of untidiness by the age of twenty-two. Fewer still, perhaps, had come from families who in three generations had managed to acquire an aura almost of royalty around their public image and whose skeletons had hitherto been concealed in elegant, eighteenth–century cupboards. Yet here she was, perfectly at ease and evidently unaware of the fact that Jack's eyes were popping out of his head every time he glanced her way.

It was a phenomenon to be taken into account, since, although Mrs Parkes could be counted upon to remain immune to all blandishments, I could not feel so sanguine about her husband. I had only to remember the regularity with which Ellen was presented at the end of every visit with a bunch of his most precious and jealously guarded flowers to see him already as a broken reed in the coming conflict.

In the meantime, it was up to me to find out all I could about her, in the hope that some of it would show her in an unattractive light, and, plunging into the first gap in the conversation, I said:

'Toby tells me you're writing a play.'

'That's right.'

'How's it going?'

'Sort of going and not going,' she replied in her muttery way, as though suffering from incipient lockjaw.

'There is no need to be modest,' Toby assured her. 'Sometimes when actresses ask that question they mean "Is there a part for me?" but it is not so in Tessa's case, she is simply curious.'

'I'm never modest,' Rosie said, sounding surprised by the suggestion. 'And there'd certainly be a part for Tessa, if she wanted it. She's so terrific I bet she could play any old part, if she really wanted to.'

Round one to Rosie and I retired to my corner to freshen up for the next bout, leaving the conversation to continue without me.

'I won't ask you what it's about,' Toby said. 'Not being modest, you might conclude that I at least had an ulterior motive.'

79

'Which, in his case, would be true,' Jack warned her. 'So beware!'

'Is that right? Then I will tell him, because, whatever else, he'll listen.'

'On your own head,' Jack said, taking a pipe from one pocket of his pink and grey tweed suit and a tobacco pouch from another. He always smoked cigars in London and a pipe in the country.

'It's about a man living alone on a remote desert island,' Rosie began. 'We learn that he has been there over a year, so far as he can tell from a sort of calendar he checks off at every sunrise, and that he landed up there because of being on the run from the law. So he opted for this other kind of prison and, since he's an intellectual and everything and resourceful too, he's brought along a crateful of books, including manuals on fishing and carpentry and stuff like that, as well as lots of philosophy and poetry.'

'Not to mention his eight favourite records, presumably. How do we learn all this? Does he talk to himself?'

'That's right! Well, I mean, you would, wouldn't you? But, naturally, it doesn't all come pouring out like I've told you. We only learn it gradually and I'll explain how in a minute. First of all there's something else you need to know about him. When he first arrived on the island his wife was with him, or she may have been his girlfriend, that's not important. The thing is that about six months ago she disappeared.'

'Does he tell us what happened to her?'

'No, it's a mystery. It's the crucial bit of the plot. The opening scene has him sighting a small boat through his field glasses. He can tell it's making a straight line for the island and it sends him into a panic. So he starts stumbling about and talking to himself and wondering aloud whether it's something to do with this woman, or whether they've finally caught up with him for whatever crime it was he'd committed. I think that would be a natural reaction, don't you? Anyway, Scene One ends with him seeing them drop anchor, or whatever it is they do, a few yards off shore and then three people walking up the beach towards the hut. It might be cut down to two in the final version because of keeping the costs down. What do you think, so far?'

'I am keeping an open mind,' Toby said, although, as far as I could see, this was only true in the sense that a rabbit keeps an open mind about the snake who has chosen to mesmerise it. Rosie's undivided attention had been focused on him ever since the curtain went up on her play and she had moved her chair a few inches closer to his, seemingly to spare herself the need to raise her voice above its normal low hum. They were now virtually inhabiting a desert island of their own, with me as passive observer and Robin and Jack carrying on a desultory, haphazard attempt at conversation on my other side. There was no longer any point in worrying about Mrs Parkes's ability to remain ruthless to the end, or the possible defection of Mr Parkes. It had become clear that any weak link in the chain of defence was more likely to be provided by Toby than either of them.

'Shall I go on?' Rosie asked, but I did not hear the answer because, by an odd coincidence, Mrs Parkes entered the room at this point and advanced a few steps towards me, fixing me with a meaningful glare, the exact meaning of which was revealed by her saying:

'You're wanted on the telephone.'

As the only telephone in the house was in the hall, a few yards from where I was sitting, and had not rung for at least an hour, we both knew her statement to be untrue, but I stood up at once and followed her out of the room and into the kitchen.

'Does that one mean to stay all night?' she asked.

'That may be her intention,' I admitted. 'Want me to try and thwart her?'

'If you would. It's past eight o'clock, you see, and Mr Crichton told me dinner not later than eight fifteen because Mr Pullborough's got an early start in the morning.'

'So has Robin,' I said, 'and he and I have to get all the way back to London before we go to bed. So I tell you what, Mrs Parkes, why not just bounce in when you're ready and round us all up? Rosie may be shamed into taking her leave, or she may allow herself to be persuaded to stay for dinner, but at least the rest of us won't be kept hanging about.'

'That's just what I would have done, only I can't, see! I could eke out the soup with a bit more stock, but there's no way I know of to make four Dover sole go round for five people. Not in this day and age,' she added regretfully, inspired, no doubt by the reflection that these things had been better ordered two thousand years ago.

'Then I'll just have to make the big sacrifice. When you bring the fish in, slap a plate of cold ham and salad, or something, in front of me and I'll pretend I have to knock off four pounds in a week otherwise I'll lose my chance to play the anorexic I'm up for.'

'Well, yes, I suppose that might be best, though it seems a shame you should be the one to suffer just because no one's got the spunk to tell that Rosie a thing or two about manners. If you ask me, she's the kind who'll stop at nothing, if she's allowed to get away with it.'

'My opinion too and, if you ask me, you'll need to keep a sharp watch on that one, Mrs Parkes.'

As it turned out, though, no sacrifice was required from me on that occasion. Mrs Parkes duly made her entrance to announce that dinner would be ready in five minutes, if that suited us. Robin and Jack beamed at her in a way to suggest that it suited them down to the ground and Rosie, after a quick glance at the assembled company, came to a decision which brought her to her feet, whereas Toby, after a momentary hesitation, responded to the situation in a manner so untypical of him as only to be compared with the sun rising in the west.

'Won't you join us, Rosie?' he asked.

'Love to,' she replied, 'but better be off. This talk of food has reminded me that my son probably thinks it's about time for his dinner too. Poor Brian will be having a hell of a time with him. It's a shame you're going to London tomorrow, though. I'd awfully like to tell you about my second act. It's the one that bothers me most.'

'Never mind,' he said, sending further shock waves through his hearers, who included Mrs Parkes, still awaiting her instructions, 'it's only for one night.'

'Oh, great!' Rosie said, gathering up her hold-all, which was the size of a junior portmanteau. 'Bye, Jack, lovely to see you. Bye, Robin. And goodbye, Tessa. It's been fabulous to meet you at last and quite a relief, in a way.'

'Really? Why's that?'

'Oh, because my old Gran's always singing your praises and what a pity I don't try to be more like you. I do begin to see that she may have a point.'

It was blatant, admittedly, but as, in my view, the essence of flattery lies in the implication that one is worth the effort of flattering, I was none the less gratified.

'Just right,' Toby said, laying his hand against the bottle of wine and leaving an imprint on its thin coating of vapour, 'I think we'll need a coaster, though.'

'Isn't it on the table? I'm sure I put it out.'

'Well, look for yourself, Mrs Parkes, because I can't see it.'

'That's funny,' she said, opening and shutting some of the sideboard cupboards and drawers in a somewhat tempestuous manner, 'and it doesn't seem to be here either. I wonder now— '

'What do you wonder?'

'Oh, never mind. I'll just fetch a cork mat, to be going on with.'

'What do you wonder, Mrs Parkes?' Toby asked again, when she returned a minute or two later.

'Well, I wasn't going to say anything. None of my business, I daresay, but I didn't like the look of him.'

'Who is him?'

'That chap with the beard. Brian something.'

'Has he been here this evening?'

'About half an hour ago, when I was out in the kitchen. "Hello," I thought to myself when I saw him, "I wonder what you're up to, my lad?" '

'But you didn't say it to him?'

'Didn't get a chance. He walked past the window, where I was standing by the sink and when I went to the back door to see what he wanted, he'd vanished. So I took it he'd walked in through the side door and found you all in the drawing room. It slipped my mind afterwards, what with the telephone call and everything.'

'And you think he might have turned left instead of right and removed the coaster from this table?'

'Well, not for me to say, is it? You'd better ask the Inspector what he thinks about it. I'll bring the fish now, if you're all quite ready.'

< 2 >

'Full marks to Mrs Parkes, wouldn't you say?' I enquired on the journey back to London. 'She took in the situation during the two minutes she spent watching Rosie at work and went into action. By the time we got to the dining room the coaster had gone.'

'You imply that she removed it herself?'

'Oh, without a doubt and then invented the fairy tale about seeing Brian go past the window. Clever thinking, in my opinion. As we both know, it's not unheard of for Toby to be knocked sideways by some young woman who's going flat out to make a donkey of him. In our complacency, we imagined he'd grown too old and wise to be caught like that again, but Mrs Parkes knew better. She guessed that nothing would dampen the fires more effectively than the knowledge that the young woman's lover was popping round whenever he felt like it and helping himself to the Georgian silver.'

'Although you have no proof that she made the story up.'

'I don't need it. She is not one to mislay an article of that nature, or to imagine she had put it out on the table when she hadn't. Furthermore, Brian may be a petty thief and several other undesirable things as well, but I doubt if even he would leave a tiny child alone in an isolated cottage at seven thirty in the evening.'

'So, presuming you're right, what do you suppose Mrs Parkes proposes to do next?'

'Bide her time and see which way the cat jumps, I expect. There's no hurry. Toby won't make a move in any direction, or even refer to the matter. He has an absolute phobia about being mixed up in some local scandal. If his burgeoning infatuation hasn't been nipped in the bud by this episode, she'll have to think of something else. If it works, I imagine she'll sit tight and not refer to it again either.'

'I wonder,' Robin said.

'What?'

'How she knew where her victim's weak spot was located and so was able to put the knife straight in. You didn't tell her about Brian's reputation, did you?'

'No, certainly not. As though I would! And I have to

admit I see what you mean. That does put rather a new slant on the affair, doesn't it?'

'So perhaps, after all, you maligned her. She really did see Brian walk past the window and he really did nick the coaster.'

'Although, if so, I can't understand why he had to be so conspicuous about it. Unless of course he's a raving kleptomaniac. Oh well, another of life's mysteries and, in the meantime, how's the main story coming along? Has Conrad arrived yet?'

'I imagine so. He was due in this morning, so he may have been able to clear up some of the confusion by now. The inquest had already been postponed until such time as he could get here.'

'And he'll be in time for the funeral too, which is on Wednesday, as you know. Will you be able to get there?'

'Shouldn't think so for a moment.'

'Never mind, it'll be very quiet. More or less family only, according to Candida. Not that quiet is exactly the word one would pick to describe that lot.'

'But you'll be there?'

'Yes, I seem to have got myself into the position of being more or less family myself at the moment. Perhaps I'll ask Ellen to stand in for you.'

'Why on earth would she want to do that?'

'I don't suppose she'd want to, but I may need her. Venetia is bound to be among those present, wouldn't you say?'

'No idea. Who's Venetia?'

'Oh, come on, Robin, you're not concentrating. Venetia is Jeremy's sister, who is married to someone called Alec Henderson, who is related to Conrad. So they are sure to be there and what more natural, when we all straggle out of the Church, than Ellen stopping to say hello to her sister-in-law?'

'Oh, I've got it now. Your game is to wangle an introduction to Conrad.'

'Quite so and I should think I'm more likely to find him in that company than among the more or less family, wouldn't you say? Obviously, there's no love lost there, quite apart from the fact that his mother-in-law is now busily putting it around that he murdered Eliza by remote control.'

'Though it's to be hoped he doesn't know that yet.'

'He could well be about to find out, or, at any rate, start putting two and two together. I have a feeling that Evadne was not altogether dissatisfied with my reception of her wild theory. Only to be expected, since I was egging her on to even greater excesses, but, if so, she may not have wasted a minute in passing it on to a higher quarter. Do you suppose they'd take it seriously?'

'No, it would have been such a reckless hit and miss way to commit murder. Still, I daresay they might feel obliged to probe a little deeper before dismissing it out of hand. Your own judgement will be based on different criteria, no doubt. You will keep him under close scrutiny for not less than two minutes, by the end of which you will be able to state categorically whether he could, or could not, have killed his wife.'

'I am not sure that it will be quite so simple as that,' I replied, pretending to take him seriously, 'but it is good to know that you have such faith in my powers of perception. It will give me confidence.'

EIGHT

Toby arrived in time for tea the following afternoon, with the intention, judging by the size of his suitcase, of remaining for at least two nights. I concluded that, so far, Mrs Parkes's policy was paying off and that it would be superfluous to enquire whether the coaster had turned up.

He told me that he had driven up with Jack and had taken him to lunch at his club.

'Wasn't that rubbing salt in the wound?' I enquired.

'In what way?'

'I thought it was well known that Jack had been lobbying for years to become a member of your club? It must have been galling for him to lunch there with a lowly client.'

'Not at all, I was doing him a favour. The more often he's seen there, the more people will get the impression that he's a member already and the battle will be half won. However, I must admit that wasn't my motive today. We were lunching with Denis Hungerford, who is trying to pull a fast half dozen and I needed the security of familiar surroundings and a waiter, at least, who was on my side.'

'You mean Jack wasn't?'

'In theory he was there to protect my interests, but in practice, as we all know, he'd be on whichever side was likely to provide the best deal for himself. And don't ask me why I don't take my custom elsewhere, because we've been through all that before. Jack does me enough damage as my friend, God knows what he'd be like as an enemy.'

'What interest was he supposed to be protecting today?'

'Denis is doing a television version of *Pieces of Eight*. Didn't I tell you that?'

'Yes, you did and I thought it was all set up and fees and royalties agreed on?'

'Oh, indeed! Jack has no equals in that department. It's a question of the screen adaptation. Denis asked me if I wanted to do it myself, but I said no. Unlike some, I do know my own limitations.'

'Not to mention your own boredom threshold. Do go on!'

'The upshot is that he's hired some tiresome woman no one except himself has ever heard of. He sent me the first draft last week and I was never more shocked in my life. It's an absolute travesty, with most of the best lines either cut or put into a different context and everyone keeps going for country walks, or into the kitchen to wash up. The only reason for my characters walking or washing up is that I need to get them off stage for a few minutes. In this version we not only see them at it, but have to listen to some very unfunny extra dialogue.'

'What is the name of this female philistine?'

'How should I know? And, if I did, I should try to put it out of my mind. I really wanted Rodney Blakemore to do it, as I told Denis all along. He's not brilliant, but he doesn't have illusions about possessing creative talent, which is the millstone of that industry.'

'And what has he got against Rodney?'

'The last thing you'd expect. I'm sure he's lying, but he's trying to fob me off by pretending Rodney's not available. I don't know what that means. He's perfectly capable of turning in a respectable job on a thing like this in a couple of weeks.'

'I wouldn't be too sure about that, Toby. In fact, I believe Denis may have got it right this time. I doubt if he'd be willing to take on any other work just now.'

'What on earth makes you say that?'

'Something he was telling me the other day.'

'I didn't know he was a friend of yours. Since when?'

'Oh, we've known each other on and off for years, but the weird thing is that he's lurched into my life in quite a big way recently. Perhaps it was Meant,' I said, laying heavy emphasis on the last word and, being as superstitious as I am and very respectful of signs and portents, he was inclined to be impressed:

'You may be right.'

'You bet I am. Whenever things are not going your way, put your faith in the supernatural. Just think how often, when you've been trying to get hold of someone or other, the telephone rings and, bingo, there they are on the line.'

His expression had now changed to one of doubt and suspicion and I realised I had chosen the wrong example. Whenever the telephone rings in Toby's house and there is no one but himself to answer it, his policy is to let it ring.

Robin took a different line:

'How's the local burglar coming along?' he asked when he joined us half an hour later. 'Any more valuables disappeared since we last saw you?'

'No, nothing to speak of,' Toby replied, looking a trifle put out.

'Do you imply that you have lost something too trivial to be worth mentioning, or so precious that you can't bear to speak of it?'

'I haven't lost anything at all, so far as I am aware, but it appears that someone else may have.'

'May have?'

'There are two schools of thought.'

'Oh well, that makes a change. What is it and who may have lost it?'

'According to Mrs Parkes, who, as you know, is well up in these matters and also has a friend appropriately named Mrs Daly, Angela Simonson has lost an emerald ring.'

'What is so appropriate about the name?'

'The fact that she is employed by the Simonsons every weekday as personal maid, laundress and valet. This, as you can imagine, brings her into close and regular contact with both of them and makes her a party to many secrets of the boudoir, most of which, as far as I can make out, she passes on with all speed to Mrs Parkes.'

'But what could be secret about losing an emerald ring? Tessa is beginning to gain a reputation for discretion, but I can't see her carrying it to those lengths.'

'I am at a loss to understand how she gained it in the first place.'

'Stop fooling about,' I said. 'Just tell us about Lady Simonson's ring. Was anything else stolen?'

'No, nothing. Her story is that the last time she remembers wearing it was when she went to the supermarket in Storhampton.'

'How typical!' I remarked. 'It was probably kept specifically for that purpose. I remember once admiring a pearl necklace she was wearing and she said "Oh, my dear, these are only my morning pearls." I suppose the ring was insured?'

'For countless thousands, no doubt, but Robert is refusing to claim.'

'And that's most untypical. Why is he?'

'This is where the great secret comes in and where we

91

have Mrs Daly dashing away with her smoothing iron and just happening to overhear a conversation between Robert and his wife, in which he accuses her of being a cheat and a liar.'

'My goodness, the things that go on behind these neo-Georgian façades!'

'Mrs Daly was shocked beyond measure, almost scorched one of his silk shirts. So far as she could follow it, something of this kind has happened once or twice before and on the last occasion, involving a gold watch, the insurance man seems to have gone beyond the call of duty in asking awkward questions. After about an hour of it Angela lost her nerve and suddenly recollected having left herself short of cash after a shopping expedition in London. Whereupon she had nipped into a pawnbroker's shop, which happened to be handy and exchanged the watch for a couple of hundred or so, to pay for her lunch and a taxi home afterwards. A likely tale, say Mrs Daly, Mrs Parkes and Robert in one voice.'

'So what, in their view, is she likely to have done with it?'

'In a word, flogged it.'

'But I thought the Simonsons were supposed to be rolling?'

'He is, she isn't. He's very jealous and keeps her on a tight rein. I'm on her side, in that respect. If she is really selling off her jewellery in order to salt something away for a rainy day, she has my full support.'

'Although I suppose she denies it?'

'With her last breath, while simultaneously justifying it, on the grounds that one of these days he'll leave her destitute and go bouncing off with someone else.'

'I am not surprised', Robin said, 'that you don't waste time hobnobbing with your neighbours. You must learn far more about them this way than you ever would at their own dinner tables.'

'You are quite right, my dear, and some of it can provide useful copy. Mrs Daly has even come up with a workable curtain line for Act One.'

'Oh, really? Do tell us!'

'According to her and as relayed to me by Mrs Parkes, Angela's presentiment of being left on the scrap heap to starve is all too well founded and the most heavily backed to see her off at present is Rosie Deverell.'

'One thing is becoming clear,' I told Robin later that evening, when we had all retired to our own apartments, 'if Machiavelli were operating today, Mrs Parkes would have been recruited on to his staff years ago. If anything could be more repugnant to Toby than the thought of his house being infested with layabouts and burglars, it would be the image of himself as a rival to that vulgar philistine, Robert Simonson.'

'You consider her tale about him and Rosie to be another calculated flight of fancy?'

'Not necessarily, but it doesn't make much difference whether she made it up, or was simply repeating the gossip, the important thing was to get it through to Toby. As a matter of fact, it wouldn't surprise me if it were true.'

'How strange! From the little I know of Simonson, I find it hard to believe. I understood his interest in young women was confined to the beautiful and brainless, some of whom, including Angela, he ended by marrying. I wouldn't have put Rosie in that category.'

'Not bad looking, though, is she? And I'm sure she's capable of putting on an act of inanity when the occasion demands. In fact, I begin to suspect her of being one of those females who were born with the gift of being all things to all men. Something Nana told me prompted that idea.'

'What was that?'

'She said that a few evenings ago Rosie had turned up and dumped the baby on her for several hours. She explained that she had an appointment which she couldn't take the child to and Nana described her as being very smartly turned out, so much so that she hadn't recognised her at first.'

'All of which led you to believe that she was on her way to meet some man?'

'Well, she certainly wouldn't have bothered to tart herself up and park the baby for the benefit of an old friend, so it seemed the most likely answer. Anyway, it's becoming obvious that Rosie is far from being the simple, stereotyped drop-out everyone takes her for. There is more to her than meets the eye, as we both saw when she went to work on Toby. Another interesting thing, though, was the timing of this mysterious appointment.'

'You may tell me what's interesting about it, providing you keep it short. I might be asleep in two minutes.'

'The point is that Nana couldn't remember exactly which evening last week it was. Well, it can't have been the night of the birthday party because we all know what she was up to then, and for equally obvious reasons it couldn't have been after Eliza's death. So that only leaves one evening last week and it struck me that the purpose of dressing like a normal person might have had less to do with looking smart than looking inconspicuous. That could also have been her reason for not lugging the baby along. In other words, she hoped to escape the attention of porters, reception clerks, or anyone else who happened to be around when she arrived at a London hotel and travelled up to the eighth floor.'

NINE

< 1 >

I had been curious to see how the warring factions would dispose themselves at the funeral and Ellen and I had discussed the possibilities at some length during the interminable trek to the crematorium, which appeared to be situated roughly midway between central London and the Outer Hebrides.

'My understanding is', I told her, 'that at functions of this kind the husband or wife automatically rates as next of kin. This means, incidentally, that Jeremy would take precedence over Toby, so it might be tactful of you to outlive them both.'

'OK,' she agreed, 'but I can't see what difference it makes. It's not like a wedding.'

'Nevertheless, there are certain rituals attached to it, the single wreath on the coffin, for one. Also it's the custom for the chief mourner to linger in the porch after the ceremony and say a few words to each of us as we file out.'

'Well, if Conrad has any sense he'll leave that bit to Evadne and forget about protocol. She'd be in her element and from what I hear of him he wouldn't give a damn for the conventions.'

'No, but it is the kind of thing we are here to find out. People can react in unexpected ways when they're under stress and their guards are down and I hope to get a few clues as to what kind of a man he is and whether Evadne could possibly be right about him. Oh, I say, I do believe we've arrived. And not so very late, after all, judging by the number of cars.'

This was over optimistic, however, for the verger, or whatever they're called in those places, was in the act of closing the door as we came up the steps. Appearances suggested that he meant to go on doing so until it slammed in our faces, but luckily he capitulated under the spell of Ellen's celebrated smile.

There were not more than thirty in the congregation, three-quarters of them massed together on the left of the aisle, where Evadne occupied the front pew. She was wedged between Candida and Benedick, with Cressida between him and his ex-wife, who stands out among those of my acquaintance who have re-inforced the belief that people grow up to fit their names, hers being Grizel.

The two pews behind theirs were filled with a dozen or so of the younger generation, mostly unidentifiable, the tail consisting of domestic retainers, with a sprinkling of soberly dressed anonymous people, whose demeanour suggested that they spent three-quarters of their lives going to funerals. Notable absentees were Rosie and Nana.

Ellen and I chose the unfashionable right-hand side, where there was an empty pew three rows behind the one in which Venetia sat between two men. They were immediately below the pulpit, where the preacher of the day was already installed, surveying the scene before getting down to business.

One of Venetia's escorts was a bulky man of medium age and height, with abundant hair of purest white. The other, who interested me more, partly perhaps because of my recent reflections about Grizel, was on her left and nearest the aisle. In the second or two before we all sat down I had noticed that he was exceptionally tall and thin, with a tonsure-like patch in his wispy, dark hair and fitted in all respects with the image I had created for him. In other words, whereas the first man was the embodiment of a successful Harley Street specialist, the second was the eccentric and dedicated anthropologist to the life. It was disappointing, therefore, to learn from Ellen, as we waited for Evadne and her retinue to precede us out of the chapel, that I was one hundred per cent wrong.

'Are you sure?' I asked, not best pleased.

'Well, of course I'm sure. I've met Alec dozens of times and I remember thinking at their wedding that he'd look much more suitably dressed in a cassock than morning coat and striped trousers.'

'So much for the unbeatable combination of logic and intuition,' I said. 'Come on, let's try and nab them before they get away.'

True to predictions, Evadne was holding court in the porch, under a very fetching black and white hat, and there was no possibility of cutting short her sad little speech, or of withdrawing my hand from both of hers before she was ready to release me. Luckily, however, Ellen had taken the view that her duties were now over and had already covered the fifty yards to the parking space by the time I caught sight of her again, standing beside one of the cars and talking to her sister-in-law. There was no sign of the two men though, and, even as I approached, Venetia climbed in beside the driver and the whole party drove away.

'Couldn't you have delayed them for a few moments?' I asked, as we walked towards our own car.

'Only by brute force and I didn't consider that necessary at this stage.'

'I don't know why not. God knows what other stages there are likely to be. Did you get a chance to talk to him at all?'

'Just "hello", you know, and all that. He's quite attractive.'

I was impressed, not to say slightly stunned by this verdict. So far as I had been aware, since the day of her first setting eyes on Jeremy, she had scarcely noticed the existence of any other human male and it seemed to me that, in awakening such a response, Conrad had proved himself to be a rare one and no mistake. I felt crosser than ever to have missed by such a hair's breadth the chance of meeting him myself.

'Which is why', Ellen continued, in her calm, unhurried way, 'I invited Venetia to bring him and Alec for a drink this evening.'

'You did what? No, don't bother to repeat it, I heard you perfectly. Did she accept?'

'Oh, you bet. She said it would be such bliss to see her little brother, which is her irritating way of referring to Jeremy.'

'How about the other two?'

'Oh, they'll come, never fear. Conrad has appointments with various people this afternoon, mainly connected with his work, I gather and the plan was that they'd meet somewhere at about six and then drive down to Windsor. I am sure Alec would settle for a free drink any day of the week and Conrad won't have much choice because he's staying with them. In any case, Venetia will see to it. She told me she quite dreaded having to spend another whole evening with him. She finds him a bit overpowering. If you're free this evening, why not join us? Six makes such a good number, I always say.'

'I don't recall you saying it before and, as you're well aware, no power on earth would keep me away. The only snag is— '

'If you mean Robin, why not add him to the list? Seven can be a good number too, in its way.'

'No, not Robin, he never expects to find me bending over the hot slippers. The snag is Rodney. I promised to give him a graphic account of the funeral and he's coming this evening. The trouble is that I need to keep on good terms with him just now because there's a little business of your Pa's that I want to sound him out about.'

'You could ask him to come here instead?'

'That's very kind of you, Ellen, but something tells me that, although he'd be as riveted as any of us by coming face to face with Conrad, I can't see seven being a very good number if it included Rodney. We'll have enough cross currents whizzing about, without his contribution. No, I'll just have to think of a tactful way of putting him off till tomorrow.'

'OK, Tess, whatever you say. They're invited for six fifteen, so try not to be late.'

< 2 >

It was as well that the glimpses I had caught of Conrad at the chapel should have prepared me for meeting him head on, for he was so unlike the demon of Evadne's description that I might either have laughed aloud, or stared at him in disbelief.

He and the rest of his party arrived a few minutes after me and, having worked through the introductions, Ellen, with masterly stage management, installed Venetia in a chair so close to Jeremy's that she was practically sitting in his lap, then turned the full radiance of her smile on Alec, saying how jolly it was to see him again and that she had been wondering ever since their last meeting exactly what he had meant by something or other, leaving Conrad no choice but to take the empty seat beside mine.

I had been pondering the form my opening remarks should take, whether to dispose at once with a few conventional words on the subject of Eliza's death, or to wait for some sign from him before introducing it, but this proved to have been a waste of time. He had hardly lowered himself to the point where his face was on a level with mine before saying:

'Venetia tells me you're an actress. I guess I was supposed to know that without being told, but I haven't been back to this country for four or five years now and I'm out of touch. I expect you knew my wife, Eliza, didn't you? You'd be a good bit younger than her, but she was on the stage too for a time.'

However, before I could answer he was on his feet again and leaping across the room, somewhat in the manner of an overweight gazelle, to gather up a bowl of nuts and, after re-seating himself, to scoop up a generous handful. I had assumed that the purpose had been to give me time to change gear and take in the fact that condolences would not be welcomed, but in fact he explained it by saying that he had been too much on the go all day to find time for lunch and life in the bush for the past eight years had left him with the habit of eating whatever happened to be available whenever he got the chance.

'And did your wife fall into those ways too?' I asked, hoping to hit the right note. 'Before you answer, though, I must tell you that I never met her, although I wish so much that I had.'

'Yes, I wish you had too. She was an extraordinary woman in lots of ways.'

'It will be hard to adapt yourself to living out there without her, I imagine.'

He paused, his hand already half-way to his mouth with a fresh consignment of nuts, then changed course and tossed them back in the bowl, saying flatly:

'I should imagine so too. It hadn't occurred to me to put myself to the test. I never had the slightest intention of going back there without Eliza.'

'Oh, I see. Forgive me, I should have realised how impossible it would be for you, but you seemed so— '

'So what?'

'I find it difficult to express without sounding even more insensitive. It was just that you appeared to have yourself so firmly under control and also, having heard about your dedication and single-mindedness, I thought perhaps your work might be a, well, not consolation exactly, but way of blotting out other thoughts and memories. I'm sorry if I offended you.'

'No, you haven't offended me in the least, Tessa. I am rather touched by your concern; curious too. In fact, I wouldn't half mind prolonging the conversation, only this wouldn't be quite the time and place for it, do you think?'

'Not quite, no.'

'So how about having lunch with me tomorrow?'

'I thought you were staying down in Windsor.'

'So I am, but I wasn't suggesting you should come there. I still have some business to settle in London and tomorrow would be as good a day as any. One o'clock at the Ritz suit you?'

'Thank you, I shall look forward to it.'

Ellen and Alec, who had left the room a few minutes earlier, now returned, each bearing a dish of smoked salmon canapés, the larger of which Ellen set down on the table in front of Conrad.

'I made these before you came,' she explained, 'and then forgot all about them. Do help yourself.'

Seeing this as the signal for a game of general post, I gave up my place to her on the sofa and ambled over to endear myself to Venetia by telling her what a fantastically stunning dress she was wearing.

'Instant conquest,' Ellen said when the Windsor party had left and Jeremy had retired to his study to put through a few mergers and take-over bids before dinner. 'I noticed you had struck up quite a *rapport*, but I hadn't realised he'd made as much progress as that. He's a fast worker, I'll say that for him.'

'You are quite mistaken,' I told her, 'in inferring that his attentions had anything to do with me, personally.'

'He has a funny way of not showing it.'

'Shall I tell you what my theory is?'

'Yes, do!'

'That his dependence, or whatever you care to call it, on Eliza was based on companionship as much as anything else. And, after all, why not? They could never have stuck that life as long as they did without each other's company and she was probably well above average in wit and intelligence. It would account for his decision not to return to the island without her and, if you ask me, what he misses most just now is some female to listen and encourage him to talk about himself. With all her virtues, one couldn't expect much in that line from Venetia and I just happened to be around to act as audience. It could just as easily have been you, or any number of other women who happen to be familiar with these particular ropes. Don't you agree that's the whole, complete answer?'

'Well, perhaps not the whole one, no.'

'Really, Ellen, it's not like you to be obstinate. What's the objection?'

'Mainly that it's based wholly and completely on what I believe is called hearsay in Robin's circles. Your only reason for assuming that Conrad relied so heavily on Eliza is that Evadne told you so. And yet in the next sentence you say that she was capable of making up any old thing in order to throw suspicion on him. For all you know, they were becoming bored stiff with each other and one reason for coming to London was to start proceedings for a divorce. I don't say that's any more likely to be true than Evadne's version, but he certainly doesn't look to me like a man whose life has just collapsed in ruins. Actually, he doesn't look exactly like my idea of a murderer either, but that's another prejudice, so you may discount it, if you wish.'

'I mean to, since I am told on good authority that as a breed they vary quite widely, but the one thing they nearly all have in common is in not looking like one. However, I do see how illogical it was of me to accept Evadne's word as gospel and I'm obliged to you for pointing it out. I must try to keep an open mind.'

'Which won't prevent you from keeping the lunch date too?'

'No, why should it? No point in having an open mind unless you can find something to fill it with, specially as he seems to be the one who's so eager to do it.'

'And will you tell Robin?'

'Yes and Toby too, if he's interested. Which reminds me that they'll both be at home by now and I'd better whizz off and start ministering to their needs.'

Ellen shook her head: 'Not Dad. He'll be on a train to Storhampton by now. Sorry about that. I was meant to tell you as soon as you arrived, but so much has been happening that I forgot all about it.'

'Did he say why?'

'I couldn't quite make it out. Apparently, Mrs Parkes rang up to say something had gone wrong with the heating

103

apparatus in the pool and Mr Parkes has had to drain all the water out before they can come and fix it. For some unfathomable reason, Dad appears to think that this necessitates his presence at home.'

'It is not entirely unfathomable to me, but there isn't time to explain now. Say good night to Jeremy for me and I'll call you as soon as I have any news.'

< 3 >

After all, Robin was not waiting for me when I arrived at Beacon Square some twenty minutes later, although someone else was. Luckily for my delicate nerves, however, the clues to this discovery had been laid thickly enough to blunt the shock.

The first thing my eye lighted on as I opened the front door was a battered old carrier bag, stuffed to its limits with an open package of something called Kosinapps sticking out of the top of it. The second was a message on the pad by the telephone, which is always my first port of call when I have been absent from home for more than ten minutes. It was from Mrs Cheeseman and read as follows: 'Have put the young lady in the drawing room. She said she was Lady Devvil's grandaughter, so thought it would be all right. The Inspector rang to say he would be late home and not to wait dinner.'

Rosie had removed her walking shoes and was reclining on the sofa, reading the *New Yorker*. Ned was asleep in an armchair, the teat of a half-empty bottle of orange juice resting against his chin, having presumably dropped from his mouth when he passed out, and I was somewhat bothered to notice that the blanket he was wrapped in looked suspiciously worn and thin.

'It's OK,' his mother said, swinging her legs down and the rest of herself upright in one flowing movement, 'he's swathed from neck to toe in waterproof plastic, so your cushions are safe.'

I found myself thinking that if she had been lounging about reading the *New Yorker* in someone else's house I should have been almost pleased to see her.

'Would you care for a drink?' I asked, busying myself with bottles and glasses and checking that Mrs Cheeseman had remembered the ice.

'No thanks, I helped myself to some lemon stuff while I was waiting. Hope you don't mind? I don't make a habit of barging in on people like this,' she went on, as I returned with something more fortifying for myself, 'but I was pretty desperate.'

'Have you been waiting long?'

'About an hour. Your cleaning lady let me in. She was just leaving, but she said you were expected back any time between seven and eight thirty and it would be all right to come in.'

'Yes, of course, but why didn't you telephone to let me know?'

'I did try, but I couldn't find you under Crichton and I'd forgotten your husband's name.'

'But you did know our address?'

'That's right. Before you arrived yesterday Mr Crichton had been telling Jack about you and your husband coming for dinner and Jack wanted to know what you were doing now and everything and he asked where you lived. Mr Crichton told him you had this gorgeous house in Beacon Square and Jack was fairly impressed and wanted to know the number because the north side is twice as expensive as the south, or it may have been the other way round, I can't remember and Mr Crichton said he couldn't tell him because he never travelled about London with a compass, so it was all quite funny really and it sort of stuck in my mind.'

'Right, so now we've got that sorted out let's go on to the next bit. You said you were desperate.'

'That's right. It's my blinking car, you see. I was on my way home about two hours ago and the bloody engine just died on me. I don't know the first thing about the inside of cars and there was Ned in the back, squeaking and bellowing, and I just couldn't think what to do.'

'Must have been awful. How did you manage in the end?'

'Oh well, one or two people got out of their cars and tried to help me, but after about twenty minutes getting nowhere the cops turned up and told me I'd have to get someone to tow me away. They were quite decent about it, I will say, and when I explained about not being able to leave Ned alone in the car, one of them stayed behind to look after him and the other one came with me while I rang up my father's garage. That's when I tried to find your number, but, like I say, it wasn't in the book.'

'Why me, though? Surely your grandmother's house would have been nearer?'

'That's right, but that was the last place I'd want to go to. You can't imagine the scenes and hysteria there ever since Eliza was gathered. Or maybe you can. Anyway, I wasn't in the mood for them just then.'

'OK, I can see that, but couldn't you have taken a taxi to Paddington and waited for the next train?'

'I didn't have any money. Well only about a pound, or something, which would have got me as far as the Kensington High Street.'

'And certainly not enough to have brought you all the way back to Westminster. So what did you do? Get on a bus and then walk, or . . . Oh no, don't tell me, I can guess. Those decent policemen brought you all the way?'

'That's right. I explained about not having any money

because I'd been planning on going straight home and when they heard where I was making for, they said "Hop in!" and then waited outside until the front door was opened and I went in.'

'Yes, I'm sure they did, but if you won't think me inquisitive, it still doesn't explain why you chose to come here.'

'Oh well, you know, I remembered how Mr Crichton had said he'd be going back to Roakes this evening and I thought if he hadn't left yet I might be able to cadge a lift. I get the impression I'm too late, though?'

'Yes, I'm afraid you are. He drove up with Jack and he's gone back by train, a bit earlier than he'd expected. Some domestic crisis turned up.'

'Have they had a burglary, or something?'

'No, nothing like that. What made you think so?'

'Just it's the kind of thing that does happen when the owner's away.'

'Very true and sometimes it comes in epidemics. Has there been a spate of them down your way recently?'

'Not that I know of, but then I wouldn't, would I? The sort of people we mix with aren't likely to possess anything worth stealing. Well, sorry to have landed myself on you like this. If you'll be an angel and lend me ten quid, me and Ned will be on our way. I'll pay you back when I see you, or give the money to Mr Crichton, whichever you like.'

'There's no need for that,' I told her, 'because I have a better idea. I am now going to ring up our very own minicab firm. Both their drivers have been to Roakes at one time or another, so there won't be any difficulty about finding the way. You can use your last remaining pound for the tip and I'll tell them to put the rest on the slate.'

'Thanks, Tessa. My grandmother was quite right, you're a real sport.'

'Talking of the people you know at Roakes,' I said, while we waited for the taxi, 'have you come across the Simonsons yet?'

'Sort of.'

'Oh, really? Which sort?'

'Him, but not her.'

'Oh, I see. No, I don't. How did that come about?'

'The first time was three or four weeks ago, when he drove me down to Storhampton. The blinking car had let me down, as usual. Well, actually, Brian had left the headlights switched on all night, so the battery was flat. Anyway, I was hitching a lift and Robert was the first driver to stop. Most of them had gone flashing by looking like stone effigies.'

'Well, at least you ended up in the most plushy car in neighbourhood. In fact, I'm rather surprised he didn't put on the effigy face himself. I wouldn't have expected him to be the hitchhiker's friend.'

'That's right, I think he was a bit surprised himself. He told me he didn't normally stop for people, but he'd felt this strange sort of compulsion.'

'There now! How lucky! What was your response to that, in case it ever happens to me?'

'I told him he probably needed help and he'd recognised me as someone who could give it to him.'

'Jolly good answer! Did he agree?'

'Yes, he did.'

'Honestly, Rosie, you wouldn't be pulling my leg, by any chance?'

'Oh no, he started right off telling me how he had all these business worries and things weren't too hot at home either. Then he said he'd always hated the idea of tranquillisers and all that stuff and he'd been trying to get by with relaxation therapy, only it hadn't done much good.

When he saw me standing by the road it came over him that he'd never seen anyone looking more relaxed in his whole life and he had to know what the secret was, so I started to tell him about TM. That stands for— '

'Yes, I do know what TM means.'

'Well, Robert didn't. At least, he'd heard of it, but he imagined it was strictly for loonies. So I put him right about that and he was so fascinated that he wanted to hear more, only we'd reached the supermarket in Storhampton by that time.'

'So?'

'So he said he'd actually been on his way to London, but what the hell and come to think of it, there was no good reason why he absolutely had to be in his office before lunch, so if I were to tell him what time to pick me up, he'd drive me back home again.'

'Well, I never did, as your old Nana would say. So that was the beginning of a meaningful friendship, I suppose?'

'Not particularly. He drops in sometimes to let me know how he's progressing, mostly on Sunday mornings when he's taking the dog for a walk. He seems OK, quite a kind man, as a matter of fact. Always bringing us strawberries and beans from his garden and he even offered Brian a job, chopping wood and cutting the grass and things like that, only Brian turned it down.'

'Not grand enough for him?'

'No, nothing like that, but he's got very high principles and he doesn't approve of the rich exploiting the poor.'

'Not many people do, but why should he feel he was being exploited? Presumably, he wasn't expected to provide his services free?'

'No, but he was jolly sure Robert would offer him less than the going rate, on account of his being unskilled and everything and that would mean keeping out an experienced man who might have a wife and family to support, so it was immoral, whichever way you looked at it.'

'Well, it seems rather a lot of fuss about chopping up a few logs, but I expect he knows best. And that sounds like your taxi. They always ring the bell as though they'd been sent to waken the dead. You carry Ned and I'll bring the rest.'

< 4 >

'You've got the pensive look again,' Robin said later that evening. 'Does it bode good or ill?'

'Hard to say. It goes against the grain to admit defeat, but I must confess that I can't make Rosie out at all.'

'Does it matter?'

'Well, she does seem to exert a mysterious power over people, regardless of age, creed or political colour. You only have to remember how she turned Toby into putty in her hands.'

'Nothing remarkable about that. Behind the carefully constructed mask of misogyny, he's one of the most susceptible men I know. Just think of those two hard-faced wives of his. No one else would have been fooled by them for an instant.'

'And you could say the same about Robert Simonson, but the point is that Rosie is quite a different proposition. Those women thought of nothing but clothes and possessions whereas Rosie goes around looking like a tramp and appears to have no acquisitive streak at all. I can't make out what her game is and yet, despite everything, I find myself liking her.'

'Why must she have any game? And come to that, why

110

should you dislike her simply for making no attempt to be other than she is?'

'Because I can't entirely believe it's genuine. Consider, for instance, that play she claims to have written. Were you paying attention when she outlined the plot for Toby's benefit?'

'No, I can't say I was. Plays don't really make much sense to me until I see them performed, and not always then.'

'Then you wouldn't have noticed, but there was something false about it. I had the feeling that she was making it up as she went along— '

'You may tell me why, if you think there's a chance of me understanding.'

'Well, for one thing, she seemed to have got all the trimmings worked out, but very few of the nuts and bolts. It was as though she were throwing in little touches as they occurred to her, but had left it to some future date to work out the plot. For instance, she could reel off details about the books this man had brought with him to the island, but she hadn't decided whether the woman he'd been living with there for a whole year was his wife or girlfriend. Now that might not have made much difference if they'd been sharing a flat in Fulham, but surely in their circumstances it would have had quite a bearing on their relationship?'

'I can see it might, yes.'

'And here's an even more glaring example. When these visitors turn up, which they do within five minutes of the curtain going up, we get no indication of where they came from, how they knew of the existence of the island, or any other damn thing. No mention of the man having sighted an ocean liner on the horizon, they just materialise out of the deep blue nowhere.'

'Yes, I agree that might take a bit of swallowing, even from the fifth row of the stalls, but perhaps it was intended to be allegorical, not realistic in any way, just some comment on the human condition?'

'Even so, it might have been a good idea to have decided whether three of these allegorical people came ashore from their allegorical boat, or only two. From a purely technical point of view, if nothing else, it is hard to see how, unless the third character goes through the action with his head in a sack, the play could have been written before this point was settled.'

'Well, I'm sure you're right, but I still can't see why it bothers you so much.'

'Only because it deepens the mystery of Rosie. Either she is naïve enough to imagine that this is the way to construct a play, or else, as seems more likely, she invented all that claptrap to grab Toby's attention, which suggests that she's not so guileless as she would have us believe.'

'And that does bother you?'

'Well, as you know, I don't take kindly to having rings run round me, specially by amateurs. I suppose it could be that she and Brian work as a team and her job is to divert attention while he carries out the snatch. Apart from that, though, I can't shrug off the nagging voice that tells me that she may know a lot more than she's telling about her Aunt Eliza's death. Any developments on that front, by the way?'

'Nothing to speak of. Conrad is here, as you know and, having identified the remains, spent a couple of hours being interrogated, but nothing useful emerged. He confirmed that one, if not the main, reason for her trip was to see a specialist about her back, but having heard Dr Henderson's diagnosis, he found nothing in it which might have induced her to take her own life. The doctor has also confirmed that, although her condition was unlikely ever to be completely cured, two or three weeks' therapy treatment at his clinic might work wonders. It seems she

112

was reluctant even to consider the suggestion, at first, but finally promised to think it over and let him know if she changed her mind.'

'So what now?'

'Well, tomorrow there'll be a rapid jig round the mulberry bush to get the inquest postponed indefinitely, but that's just a formality, really.'

'And then what?'

'Then the mighty wheels start grinding into action again.'

'Will they move any further forward, do you suppose?'

'Oh, yes, no doubt of that. I dare say those in charge have a fairly shrewd idea already of how it happened. It's just a question of digging out the evidence to back it up. It may take weeks, or possibly months.'

'Want to bet on that?'

'On what?'

'That in a couple of weeks from today the case will be all wrapped up,' I said, opening my diary as I spoke.

'OK, you're on. What are you writing down?' he asked, so I read it aloud to him:

'Saturday, fifteenth June, celebration dinner, bracket, question mark, close bracket.'

TEN

'You look tired, Rodney. Have you been overworking?'

'Other way round. Only thing that makes me tired is not having enough work.'

'Well, come and sit down and I'll give you a drink to buck you up. Why aren't you working hard enough?'

'That hidden snag I told you about,' he replied, taking a mighty swig and looking, if anything, more tired than before. 'At the back of my mind I've been waiting for it to come out of the shadows and hit me between the eyes, when it was ready to.'

'And now it has?'

'Now it has. My own fault, in a way, which doesn't make it any easier. Remember my telling you about Eliza's script and what a terrific job she'd done on it?'

'With a little help from yourself. Yes, of course I do.'

'Fact is, my contribution was mainly on the technical level. Any pro could have done as much.'

'I am sure you underestimate yourself. My impression was that your interest and encouragement were a lot more valuable than all the professional expertise in the world. Anyway, we needn't argue about it because I also recall your telling me that one or two people you'd shown it to were equally enthusiastic. So what is this snag all about?'

114

'Like I said, it's partly my own fault. What you say is true and I suppose it made me over-confident. The snag is that my judgement, as well as theirs, only covered the first seven episodes. As you know, I didn't read the final one until after Eliza's death.'

'And did it then fall apart?'

'Not exactly. That wouldn't have been possible, given the standard she'd maintained all along. The ending is just as brilliant, in its way, but the trouble is that I hadn't read it closely or analytically enough to notice a few underlying implications which have since been pointed out to me.'

'What implications?'

'An unmistakable racial bias. I have to admit it and the crushing thing is that I know I could have got it sorted out with her, if only there'd been time. In the present climate of opinion no one would touch it as it stands now.'

'Oh, what a nuisance! Couldn't you just take your fat red pencil and edit those bits out?'

'It's not that simple. It's a very cleverly crafted piece of work and it hangs together from the opening scene to the last and the last is where the message really gets across. Tacking on a new ending would detract from everything that's gone before and make a hotchpotch of the whole thing. At least, that's my view.'

'But not the unanimous one?'

'There's a movement afoot for me to have a shot at reworking the entire series, removing this element and finding another one to replace it. The trouble there is that I don't have enough faith in my own ability to make a first-class job of it.'

'I expect you're underestimating yourself again, Rodney, but if you feel strongly about it, why not hand it over to someone you do have faith in?'

He shook his head like a mutinous child, staring down at his empty glass. So dealing first with the immediate problem by giving him a refill, I then waited for him to explain:

'I can't do it, Tessa. I've thought long and hard about this and it would seem like a betrayal. If someone else took it on, he might do a competent job, but it would cease to be Eliza's. At least I was in tune with the way her mind worked. Once or twice during our last session together I had the sensation of actually seeing inside it and anticipating her reactions. No, I've made up my mind on that point. If I can't make a go of it myself, then no one else is going to have the chance to try. After all, I'm the only one now to gain by its getting off the ground, so I'll be the only loser if it doesn't work out.'

'And you may have more to lose than you realise, in my opinion. You always set yourself such high standards and, if you don't look out, you'll be kicking yourself for the rest of your life for not at least having a bash. You know what I think you should do?'

'No.'

'I think you should take it out of circulation and let it lie fallow for a bit. Tell your producer that you need three months, or whatever you consider reasonable, to do a completely revised script. Then make sure to use the first of them to work on a perfectly straightforward job, which you could do in your sleep. It'll clear your mind of all the emotional entanglements and make you see things more objectively. What do you say to that?'

Rodney had narrowed his eyes and was watching me in a speculative way and for a moment I was half afraid that his trick of seeing into other people's minds had now extended to include my own. The next moment I was certain of it, for he proceeded to bowl my middle stump by saying:

'Don't think I'm not grateful for your concern, Tessa, but one could always believe that you had a vested interest in advising me to take time out for some other job.'

116

'Oh, good gracious, no. What conceivable difference could it make to me?'

'Well, not you personally, perhaps, but I know how strong you are on family ties and I admit that you have some cause to feel slightly miffed.'

'Oh no, Rodney, that's really going too far. What can you be talking about?'

'Robin, of course. We both know perfectly well that I thrust myself on him at that macabre party and then, when he'd been generous enough to make a date to meet and discuss things, I simply faded out and let the whole thing drop. I do feel bad about it, as it happens and, for all I know, he went to a lot of trouble boning up on the information I'd asked for.'

'Then stop feeling bad about it right now,' I said. 'I can't tell you whether he went to any trouble or not, but it isn't the kind of thing to bother him in the least. Besides, in view of what had happened by the time the appointment came round, he wasn't seriously expecting you to keep it. I assure you, with my hand on my heart, that there was no flicker of resentment on his part.'

'Then I'm glad I mentioned it because it's a relief to hear you say that. Fact is, you see, I've wangled myself off that police serial I'd been working on when Eliza arrived. No hard feelings, it was a mutual arrangement and they've got a new writer lined up for it. I knew I couldn't ever get back to the frame of mind I was in when I started it, or recapture the enthusiasm.'

'But I take it that wouldn't necessarily apply to some more or less routine job, like, for example, adapting a novel or stage play? Knowing you of old, you'd put all your skills and expertise into it, but it wouldn't put any creative demands on you and you might find that at the end of it you'd got your perspective right and knew exactly how to handle Eliza's script.'

117

'It's worth thinking about, I suppose. I'll see. In the meantime, thanks for listening. God knows why you should bother.'

I did not enlighten him on this point, feeling it better to end our talk on a comfortable note. Furthermore, it is all very well to pull a few strings in the cause of family loyalty, but they are more likely to be effective in the form of silken cords than sturdy ropes.

ELEVEN

< 1 >

'So I've acquired the dubious reputation of a single-minded crackpot, have I?' Conrad asked when he had dealt with our order. 'Who can have given you that idea, I wonder? No, don't bother to answer. It won't have been Venetia because she can only manage words of one syllable and Alec never makes a statement without X-rays and written evidence to substantiate it. So that only leaves my dear, benighted in-laws?'

'Isn't it true?' I asked.

'No, as it happens. More to the point, they're in no position to know whether it is or not.'

'Although, to be fair, I suppose they could have got a hint of it from your wife?'

'Oh, I doubt it very much. Eliza was given to wild exaggeration, I grant you. It was one of the characteristics that made her such fun. She could manufacture a good story out of something as trivial as a monkey perched on the bath tub, but describing me, or anyone else, as a dedicated worker? I can't see that being her style at all. Too dull, for one thing, and it doesn't really lend itself, do you think? Once you've said that, you've said it all. If you really want to know, I think she'd have been more likely to tell her loving family that I was an idle, selfish layabout, never doing a stroke of work and having it off with every raffia-skirted maiden I could lay my hands on. Much more sensational.'

'And equally fictitious?'

'Well, leaving aside the last item which, given the moral and ethical codes of those islanders, would have had me hustled off their territory, dead or alive, in a couple of shakes, I'd say the truth lay somewhere in between.'

'What brand of moral and ethical codes? Muslim? Hindu?'

'No, it's a funny old mixture when you get close to it. Somewhere back in the last century they were converted from paganism to Christianity by one of those intrepid proselytising travellers of that era and they took to it like ducks to water. It didn't go very deep, mark you. They don't regard it as sinful for women to go around topless and the men with fig leaves, but they love the hymn singing and all that side of it and they're strictly monogamous. Very gentle, kindly people, on the whole, too. In a curious way, they have more of the true Christian spirit in their make up than a lot of us church-going Westerners and yet, underneath, the old pagan religion is just as strong as ever. They manage to run them in harness and it's one of the features which makes them so fascinating to work with. All the same, I'd like to stress that, although I enjoy my work and pity the man who doesn't, I'm certainly not one to devote all my waking hours to it. I'd pity that man too.'

'So what did you do for the rest of the time?'

'Plenty. Admittedly, we were rather short on discos and fancy restaurants, but there was a lot going for anyone who enjoyed an outdoor life. Swimming, surfing, deep-sea fishing, you name it. We set up a badminton court in our so-called garden. It wouldn't have earned high marks from the Eastbourne Sports Club, but it provided a lot of fun in the cool of the evening and the

120

local boys and girls were dead keen, once they'd got the hang of it.'

'It sounds all right for a holiday, but I don't think I could have stuck it all the year round.'

'Not many people could. I used to feel restless myself, sometimes, but Eliza was never bored and she had all manner of things going on. Ante- and post-natal courses and she used to give English classes at the one and only primary school. The pupils' ages ranged from about five to twenty-five, but that didn't matter a damn. We even managed to get a little piano installed for her. It was a bit tricky keeping it in trim in that climate, but that was another thing which brought the islanders flocking. They used to sit around on the grass outside listening to her by the hour. She was queen of all she surveyed and they worshipped the ground she walked on.'

'And then, of course, there was her writing?'

'Oh yes, that too. But you're encouraging me to talk about myself again, you know. I'm apt to do that, if I don't watch it. The knack of give and take in conversation is one thing I do regret losing during the years in the bush. It's time you told me something about yourself.'

'Oh no, it would sound dreadfully ordinary by comparison. Besides, I'm really interested to hear about Eliza. I didn't realise she was musical, in addition to her other talents.'

'I wouldn't rate it as high as that. She had a good ear and she liked trying out new things.'

'How about you? Are you musical?'

'Me? Not on your life. Just as well, perhaps. I might not have been able to bear listening to her. No, sketching became my prize hobby. Not that I knew the first thing about it when I started, but I fixed myself up with all the trappings and books for beginners and it got quite a hold on me. Some of the local boys and girls became interested too and one or two had a lot more natural talent than I did. Nothing surprising in that, of course.'

'No, I suppose not. What will become of these people when they no longer have you to stimulate and stir them up?'

'Oh, they'll get along fine. Miss me a bit at first, perhaps, Eliza too, but they're happy-go-lucky sort of people. I'll be forgotten in a few months.'

'So where do you plan to live now?'

'Oh, Australia, I expect. I've got one or two irons in the university fires over there. Family too. My mother took me out with her when I was two years old and my Dad had run off with someone else. Six months later she'd married an Australian, old friend of the people she'd been staying with, and she's never been back since. So it's as much my home as anywhere else.'

'All the same, you don't sound like an Australian.'

'Ah well, the reason for that being that I was educated over here from the age of eight and it's the way you learn to speak in those formative years which sticks. That was my mother's doing. She never wanted to come back here herself, but she insisted on an English education for me. Bit illogical, when you think of it.'

'Would you do the same with a son of your own?'

'Not on your life. My boy will have to learn to talk Strine and like it. I must say, you're a dab hand at drawing people out, aren't you? It's not a talent I'd associated with actors, but then you could say I'm biased on that subject.'

'And you're pretty good at being drawn, which is not a characteristic I'd associated with scientists.'

'I take that as a double-edged compliment, but you must blame yourself for my gassing on like this about my own affairs. It's a rare luxury. Most people in this country begin by asking you what it's like living on a desert island and then, half-way through the first sentence, they're telling you how it reminds them of the package tour they went on to Corfu. Any more questions, or do you need your full concentration for that trolley I see being wheeled in our direction?'

'No, only the will power to divert my eyes from it. How about you?'

'Same here. Let's settle for coffee, shall we?'

'So no more questions?' he asked when it had arrived.

'Only two, and the first one is: how did you discover your island in the first place? Did you just stick a pin in the map and row ashore from an ocean liner?'

'Well, no, I regret to tell you that it wasn't quite so simple as that,' he replied, evidently much amused. 'I first went there for one of the United Nations agencies who were setting up a full project in the area. I still work for them, incidentally, but only on a consultancy level. It pays well and leaves me with nine months of the year free to concentrate on what I now regard as the really important work. Second question?'

'Did you read Eliza's script?'

'Which one?'

'You mean there were several?'

'Understatement. She was forever getting seized with ideas for stories and plays and for a few weeks she'd be dashing away at them hell for leather, but I don't know that any actually got finished. She'd get bored when it wasn't going the way she'd planned and then she'd switch her attention to something else.'

'Did you read any of them?'

'Oh, sure, particularly the early ones. In those days I'd study them carefully, making notes as I went along and then I'd hand over my list of comments and criticisms, as she'd asked me to, and you know what? More often than not she'd have lost interest by then and moved on to something else.'

123

'Did she ever write anything for television?'

'Curiously enough, that was her most recent craze. It was going to be in ten episodes and then she decided to cut it down to six or eight. I read the first one and it looked to me to be as good as all her other beginnings had been, but I've no way of telling how far she got with it.'

'Someone told me she'd finished it and turned in a very skilled and professional job.'

'Then I take leave to doubt their word. I suspect the only way she could have done that would be by getting someone very skilled and professional to do the donkey work. I suppose it was one of the Deverells who told you, but then they're notoriously starry-eyed about a fellow member of the clan.'

Realising that I could not put him right on this point without naming Rodney, who might not thank me for it, I moved sideways from the subject by saying:

'You've made it clear what a low opinion you have of Eliza's family, but is it based just on your own experience, or did she go along with it?'

'Now that really is a hard one to answer.'

'But you must know, surely?'

'The truth is that the little I saw of them before our marriage didn't appeal to me, but I wasn't bothered, seeing how soon we were going to be shot of them. I suppose my prejudice, if you like to call it that, was built up over the years by what Eliza told me of her childhood and from the bits she used to read aloud from their letters. But it doesn't follow that she shared my views. She used to laugh over their petty jealousies sometimes, but back of it all they were family and above criticism. Not that we ever quarrelled over it. Keeping a quarrel going with Eliza was like trying to stop butter melting in the midday sun.'

'Which reminds me,' I said, 'did you ever meet her

niece, Rosie? She'd have been around twelve or thirteen when you married.'

'Oh yes, I met them all, one way and another. Rosie was one of the bridesmaids, I remember. What did I say to remind you of her?'

'About how hard it was to quarrel with Eliza. Rosie's the same. She has that special sort of charm which makes you like her in spite of yourself.'

Conrad remained thoughtful and withdrawn for a moment or two, giving rise to the thought that he may have resented my taking it upon myself to describe Eliza to him. However, when he did speak, it was to say:

'Then I hope I don't have to meet her, now she's grown up. Eliza and I had always hoped to have a daughter and this one sounds a bit too close to what I'd imagined she'd turn out to be like.'

'Curiously enough, she has ambitions to be a writer too, although I'm afraid she still has a long way to go.'

'Why's that?'

'Speaking as one who's had to wade through more good, bad and indifferent plays than you've had coconut dinners, she doesn't seem to realise how essential it is to work within her own knowledge and experience. Her method is to take half a dozen imaginary characters and fling them into a bizarre situation, which she has no idea how she would react to, herself. Was Eliza the same?'

'Quite the reverse. Everything she wrote came straight from life. That may have been going too far in the opposite direction, but her own had been a good deal more like fiction than reality, so she had a head start there.'

'Yes, indeed!' I agreed, debating whether to go back on my word and throw out one more question. I decided not to rush things, however. There might well be a future occasion to ask whether Eliza's experience had included a party of strangers turning up on the island, apparently from out of nowhere.

< 2 >

Later that day Toby telephoned to thank me for having him to stay and to apologise for having left with no word of farewell. He is always meticulous in such niceties, even to the point of overcoming his phobia about telephones and, when blocked in my attempts to make contact through the normal routes, I have sometimes wondered whether the quickest way might not be to send him a case of wine by express delivery. However, this time he turned out to have an ulterior motive as well.

'How's the pool coming along?' I asked.

'Not very fast, I'm afraid. It seems the pump is not working as well as it should and will have to be replaced.'

'How annoying for you, although I suppose it won't take more than a day or two?'

'That depends. The question is somewhat vexed.'

'In what way?'

'It seems that after I left here on Monday morning Parkes drove Mrs Parkes down to Storhampton to get her hair washed and she tells me that when they returned two hours later there was a bearded oaf splashing up and down without any clothes on.'

'Surely even Mrs Parkes wouldn't expect him to splash up and down fully dressed?'

'You don't understand. No clothes on is the Parkes euphemism for stark naked.'

'Oh, I see! How dreadful for her!'

'And on top of that he had the effrontery to say that he had been intending to borrow some swimming trunks from

126

me, but, finding no one at home and the house locked up, had been obliged to manage without.'

'What a nerve!'

'Yes, the situation is becoming so oppressive that I am seriously considering selling the house and moving to another neighbourhood.'

'You mustn't give in just yet. I am sure Mrs Parkes will find a way out.'

'I am not so confident. She was so incensed that I am afraid she may have lost her head this time and given way to what I can only describe as an ungovernable impulse, which is not a good sign.'

'What did she do?'

'Sent the young man packing, told Parkes to empty the pool, scrub it down with disinfectant and leave it empty until further notice. A bold decision, of course, but it leaves us what you might call high and dry.'

'Although, presumably, she doesn't regard it as a permanent solution. I expect she is just giving herself breathing space to plan the next move.'

'If so, she seems to be stuck at the moment. And now, I am told, there are predictions of a heatwave at the weekend, which will be very tragic and annoying. I suppose you wouldn't have any ideas of your own to contribute?'

'Not offhand, but perhaps Mrs Parkes and I might be able to hatch some plot between us.'

'I do wish you'd try. Nothing would make her admit it, but I believe she has a sneaking respect for your talents in that line.'

'What line?'

'Oh, unmasking villains, making sure that good prevails over evil, all that kind of thing.'

'How flattering! Perhaps I'll drive down for lunch tomorrow.'

'You'll be most welcome.'

'In the meantime, Toby, have you spoken to Rodney yet?'

'No, I'm leaving all that to Jack. Jumping about and doing my bidding is what he's paid for, after all.'

'Paid or not, it doesn't follow that he'll earn it. He might think there'd be more in it for him by doing Denis's bidding this time.'

'I still don't see what I can do about it.'

'Well, how would it be if I were to bring Rodney down with me tomorrow? You could sound him out while I confer with Mrs Parkes and then, if he agrees in principle, you'll be able to tell Jack that the ground has been prepared and all he has to do is work out the terms. That might be a way to foil him.'

'Well, you have got the Mrs Fix-it persona in charge today, haven't you? How about Rodney, though? Is he likely to be available to spend a whole day in the country at a few hours' notice?'

'I don't know, but he seems to have very few social commitments at the moment and, if it came to the worst, we could always make it the day after.'

'Then you'd better find out and arrange matters with Mrs Parkes as soon as possible. She doesn't like to be kept in suspense.'

'You could hardly describe it as a cliff hanger.'

'It's about to become one. I shall have to let her know that we may be three for lunch tomorrow, or possibly two, or possibly only one and that the same applies to the next day and possibly the one after that, as well. That is the kind of suspense that unnerves her and we're in enough trouble without it.'

TWELVE

< 1 >

'Have you met Rosie Deverell?' I asked on the final stage of the journey to Roakes.

It was becoming the stock question, but had been brought out this time mainly as a means of breaking the ice, or rather widening such gaps as had appeared in it since setting out from London and whose existence was due to the fact that, instead of now inching our way towards the traffic lights at Storhampton bridge, we should have been racing up the home stretch.

This breakdown in the schedule had been brought about, as so often, by human error, the human here being Rodney Blakemore. He had accepted the invitation in a somewhat grudging fashion, saying that it would necessitate re-arranging his day and he would therefore be unable to present himself at Beacon Square until half an hour after the appointed time. This was cutting it a bit fine and freezing conditions had really set in by the time he arrived twenty minutes later still.

'I know who she is, of course,' he replied. 'Which of us doesn't, by now? Can't recall actually having met her, though. Why do you ask?'

'Just that she's living down in these parts now and she has a habit of popping up in unexpected places. The last one was about half a mile back. She was standing by the road, trying to hitch a lift, but you probably didn't notice.'

'Only in a vague sort of way, without realising who she was. Matter of fact, I thought you were going to stop for her, but then you seemed to change your mind.'

'I changed it twice. When I caught sight of her, about fifty yards ahead of us, I intended to ignore her and sweep past because, as I've already mentioned, the dragon figure of Mrs Parkes is already tapping its feet up at Roakes and we can't afford to indulge in Samaritan gestures just now. Then I realised who she was and that was different. People one knows are in a separate category and she might have waited there for hours before striking lucky with a driver who was going anywhere near Roakes.'

'But eventually you decided the dragon must have first priority?'

'No, I didn't. I remembered that, whatever else, Rosie is no fool and that is the last spot she'd have chosen if she'd really been making for Roakes. Presumably, she was on her way to Oxford or Dedley and the best I could have done would have been to drop her off in Storhampton.'

Rodney said, 'Oh well, that explains it,' with profound indifference, but then, to my surprise, added:

'You know, Tessa, there are times when I feel sorry for the rich. They must have a dog's life, in some ways.'

'Some do, no doubt, and I suppose it's possible that some of the poor do too. Who did you have in mind?'

'Your cousin, Toby, for a start. I was remembering how you went on at me about not daring to be a minute late for meals, for fear of upsetting his housekeeper. God, I'd go mad if I had to live like that.'

'Anyone would, but you've got it wrong. In the first

place, you are mistaken in supposing Toby to be a rich man. He's what you could describe as comfortably off, sometimes more comfortably than others, but never within miles of the top bracket.'

'If you say so. What else?'

'Your assumption that he pays the piper and Mrs Parkes calls the tune. Nothing of the kind. Orderliness and regularity are what suits him and Mrs Parkes makes sure he gets them. It is an ideal arrangement which they have worked out between them, without a word being said on either side.'

'I believe you,' he said, 'although thousands wouldn't.'

I felt saddened, as well as irritated by his complacency. To me, it epitomised that very lack of perception which had made him into a competent hack, rather than creative writer, since anyone who had spent half an hour in his company without realising that the wheels of Toby's existence ran firmly along the lines he had laid down for them would need to be shorter than average on human insight.

Reminded of it by these reflections, my next question was about the progress he was making on Eliza's script.

'Have you found a way round the tiresome racist snag?' I asked.

'Weren't you the one who advised me to put it aside and let it simmer for a while?'

'Yes, and I'm gratified to find you're taking my advice, but sometimes when things simmer they come to the boil when you least expect it. I just wondered whether some ideas for a solution might have popped unbidden, as they say, into your mind when you believed it was concentrating on which shoes to wear. It's at moments like those that I often get my best inspirations.'

'I wouldn't be surprised, but in my job such flights of fancy are apt to dissolve in the cold light of day. It's more a matter of slogging away and trying out different devices until you hit on the right one.'

I did not consider this attitude boded well for Eliza's posthumous reputation, but was consoled by the thought that it would suit Toby down to the ground. It was just the kind of painstaking, uninspired approach that he needed.

< 2 >

Things rarely turn out as you expect, however, far less as you would wish them to, although the dashing of these hopes was postponed until three or four hours later, when Rodney and I resumed our conversation on the drive back to London, more or less from the point where it had been left off.

Until then everything had gone smoothly, getting off to a good start with the lunch, which included an awe-inspiring steak and kidney pudding.

Toby had warned me about this in advance, saying that although he personally could eat it any old time, he was afraid our guest might find it inappropriate for a warm day in early June. However, he had been over-ruled by Mrs Parkes, who maintained that it was nice and filling and also could bear being kept back, if the guest should happen to be late.

After lunch, when the workers had retired to Toby's study, I insinuated myself into the kitchen by offering to dry the silver and glass, which were not categorised as dishwasher fodder.

'It's a nuisance about the pool,' I remarked when we were about half-way through this chore, 'specially with the weather like it is. Any idea when they'll fill it up again?'

'End of the week, they say. Might be later, might be sooner.'

'Why this vagueness?'

'All I mean is, you never can tell in this life, can you? What you need now, if you don't mind me saying so, is a fresh cloth. You'll find one in the top drawer just beside you. You'll never get the silver looking right if you keep on with that one.'

'Which reminds me, Mrs Parkes, I take it there's been no news of the missing coaster? I noticed it wasn't on the dining table.'

'That's because there hasn't been time yet to clean it up properly.'

'You mean it has turned up? Well, I'm blowed! Toby never said a word.'

'He doesn't know yet. To tell you the truth, I've been in two minds about telling him, but you might have some ideas about it.'

'I'll do my best, but first tell me where you found it.'

'It was on the Monday, the day Mr Crichton went up to London. We'd been down to Storhampton and after he'd had his dinner Parkes said he'd make a start on the lawn. That's another thing that can't always be done when Mr Crichton's at home. The noise of the mower disturbs him when he's trying to work.'

'Yes, it would. Do go on!'

'It was when he went to get the machine out of its shed that he found the coaster. It was lying just inside the door, wrapped in one of those black bags the dustmen bring. If it had been winter, it might have been lying there for months without anyone knowing.'

'How do you suppose it got there?'

'Guilty conscience, perhaps.'

'Or perhaps it was becoming an embarrassment.'

'Yes, now you mention it, I'd say that was more likely. Somebody might be on his best behaviour just now, with all this talk going round the village.'

'What talk?'

'Oh, rumours about things going missing, and a lot of it exaggerated, I dare say. You know, it starts with someone saying they've lost a bit of jewellery and it must have been stolen and the next thing is you get two or three more popping up, complaining the same thing's happened to them. It gets to the point where anyone who's left his car keys in another pocket starts going around saying this thief must have pinched them.'

'All the same, the coaster was a genuine case, so it's fair to assume that some of the others were, as well. I suppose Brian is hot favourite for the culprit?'

'Bound to be, isn't he? No denying that none of these rumours started until he and that Rosie came to live here. You saying that about it's being an embarrassment makes me think someone may have tipped off the police and they've been round there, asking awkward questions. Perhaps the young scamp was afraid they'd come back with a search warrant and was in a hurry to unload some of his ill-gotten gains.'

'Any ideas about who that someone could be? Not Toby, obviously.'

'No, you wouldn't catch him getting mixed up in it.'

'How about Sir Robert Simonson? It occurred to me, you see, that most of the stuff which is supposed to have been nicked was pretty small beer, but someone told me that Lady Simonson had lost an emerald ring. That might have been valuable enough to make him take some action.'

'Trouble there is he's certain in his own mind that his wife made up that story about the ring because she was too scared to tell him she'd turned it into cash, and he wouldn't want all that to come out.'

'He might not mind if he had the best of reasons for knowing that she hadn't done anything of the kind.'

'I don't follow you.'

'Supposing, for the sake of argument, that he'd taken the ring himself for the express purpose of incriminating someone else?'

Mrs Parkes took a minute or two to digest this theory, and when I had elaborated on it a bit she was still doubtful.

'Well, yes, I take your meaning and I daresay that's the kind of game he does get up to in the City and suchlike, but it doesn't altogether fit in here, you know.'

'You mean because he wouldn't want to do anything to distress Rosie?'

'Oh, you've heard about that too, have you? Well, yes, I suppose that would be about what I meant.'

'So in that case you could take it a stage further and say he's completely dotty about her and, being the ruthless kind, it would suit him well to get that young man seen off?'

'My word, you have got a mind, haven't you? I expect it comes from all those tales you hear from the Inspector. It's certainly not very nice to think of someone who sets himself up as gentry playing a dirty trick like that, but I daresay you could be right.'

'In which case, he'll probably get away with it, but I shouldn't worry because I can't see it doing him much good in the long run. In fact, in my opinion, the only one to benefit would be Toby.'

'Now there I don't agree. She'll still be hanging about here, with or without the young man and, if you ask me, she'd be a worse menace on her own.'

'My theory is that it's unlikely to come to that. If he finds that things are getting too hot for him here and decides to move on, she'll pack her carrier bag and go too.'

'Why would she want to do that? They're not married

and she'd have a sight more to gain by staying, if what they say about her and Sir Robert is true.'

I did not press the argument, realising that the concept that to someone as perverse as Rosie the chance of having something to gain by taking one course would be incentive enough to take the opposite one might be too much for her to swallow. Instead, I told her that I would try to find out what I could about the young couple's plans from Rosie's family, promising to keep her informed. This, however, was both more and less than the truth.

The other two had finished their business and when I emerged from the kitchen Rodney was coming downstairs on his own, carrying a script and a message from Toby to say that he proposed to join us for tea on the terrace in about an hour's time.

'That suit you all right?' I asked.

'Yes, fine, so long as I'm back in London by six.'

'Then how about a little walk to work up an appetite for tea?'

'Where to?'

'If you need an objective, I'd quite like to drop in on that girl who tried to hitch a lift this morning, to explain why we didn't stop.'

'Is it far?'

'About half a mile. Through the village and down a lane towards the valley.'

'Is there anywhere in the village where I can get some fags?'

'Yes, of course. The pub won't be open, but there's a general store and post office, where they sell everything from cup hooks to stuffed olives. You'd better leave that script in the car, as we go out, otherwise, if you're anything like me, you'll be half-way to London before you realise you've left it behind.'

'How did it work out between you and Toby?' I asked, as we walked across the Common.

'All right. Pretty good, I think, so far as it went. I still have to read it through again, but, as far as I can see, at this stage, apart from a bit of cutting there shouldn't be much more involved than breaking it down into short scenes, with camera movements.'

'The sort of thing you can do on your head?'

'If I'm allowed to. There's still Denis to contend with, don't forget.'

'Oh, I shouldn't worry about him. Toby wants you and, provided you do a good job, I can't see that he'll have a leg to stand on. There's the shop,' I added, pointing ahead of us, 'I'll go and browse through the greetings cards while you're making your purchase. They're always good fun.'

'It shouldn't take me more than a couple of minutes to buy a packet of fags, for God's sake.'

'Don't rely on it. It's as much a social club as a shop. People have been known to spend twenty minutes in there just buying a lettuce, which they then leave on the counter.'

There was another browser two or three feet away from the card racks and one whom I had least expected or desired to see, since her presence there spelt ruin for the rest of the afternoon's programme.

'Oh, hello!' I said, concealing my annoyance, 'fancy seeing you here!'

'I live here.'

'I know that, but I don't and I haven't set foot in this shop for about two years, which makes it an odd coincidence and another one is that I think I've seen you somewhere else today. Were you hitching a lift on the London road this morning?'

'That's right. I saw you pass.'

137

'Well, I wasn't being an effigy, but I didn't think you'd be standing just there if you'd been aiming for Roakes.'

'Why wouldn't I?'

'Because eighty per cent of the cars going by would be either stopping at Storhampton or else on their way to Dedley. Still, you made it, so you must have struck lucky in the end.'

'That's right. You staying down here?'

'No, only for the day.'

'I was going to say that the cottage is in a bit of a mess just now, but if you'd been able to drop by tomorrow I'd have got it tidied up a bit and I could have given you back the money I owe you.'

'Oh, no hurry about that. Next time I'm down will do.'

'Well, the thing is, Tessa, we may be moving on fairly soon.'

'Oh, why's that? Don't you like it here?'

'Yes, it's OK, but Brian gets a bit fed up, not being able to find a job and everything. Some friends of ours have found a place in Hammersmith, which is bigger than they need and we might go and share it with them.'

'Sounds all right,' I said. 'I hope it works out for you.'

Rodney, having made his purchase, had approached us during this conversation and had remained hovering near by for some minutes, but when I turned to introduce him he had disappeared. When we came out of the shop he was standing some way off, with his back to us, apparently studying the names on the War Memorial.

'Friend of yours?' Rosie enquired.

'Sort of. Would you like to meet him? He might be useful to you one of these days. Or perhaps you've got things to do?'

'That's right. Like I said, things are in a mess at home and anyway I've got to get back to Ned. Bye, Tessa, lovely to see you.'

'Any of these families still living around here?' Rodney asked, turning round as Rosie drifted away.

'One or two. The Hacketts are the local builders, very prosperous these days and there's a Mrs Daly, grandmother of those two who were killed in nineteen forty, who is quite a power in the land. Our social call is off, by the way. The house is not tidy enough to receive us, so I'll take you back through the field, if you like. That should make enough exercise for one afternoon.

'I am sorry you bustled off in that haughty way without saying hello to Rosie,' I told him, when we had walked round behind the church and through a stile into the meadow, which Toby referred to as the long cut to the village.

'Rosie?'

'The girl we nearly gave a lift to this morning. She was the one I was talking to just now and I was rather hoping to hear your opinion.'

'Oh, that one! I thought there was something vaguely familiar about her, but it was rather claustrophobic in that place and I was dying for a cigarette. Anyway, what possible opinion could I form about someone like that in a couple of minutes?'

'I thought perhaps she might have reminded you of Eliza.'

'Are you crazy?' Rodney demanded, freezing in his tracks, 'that must be just about the most inept suggestion I ever heard. She doesn't match up to Eliza in any way at all.'

'I know it sounds absurd and most people do dismiss her on sight, but once they get close and start talking to her there's a different reaction. I can't quite explain it and you lost your chance to find out for yourself, so you'll just have to take my word for it.'

'I am prepared to humour you by not arguing,' he said, starting to walk on again, 'but I can't say I'm convinced.'

'And there's something else they have in common,' I said, hoisting myself on to the five-barred gate which separated the meadow from the Common, 'Rosie is an aspiring writer, not so different in style, I would guess, from Eliza.'

'Seeing as you've never read anything by Eliza, I can't say that you're in any position to judge.'

'Well, perhaps style was the wrong word. Subject matter might have been nearer the mark. I've listened to Rosie describing a play she's working on and it's about a small group of people isolated from the world on a desert island.'

'Fancy that!' he said, pausing to light another cigarette, so I gave up the attempt to arouse a spark of interest in him and we covered the last five hundred yards to the house almost in silence.

The same glum, withdrawn mood persisted throughout the drive to London and, apart from a few random remarks about the traffic and so forth, he remained uncommunicative and lost in his own thoughts, which, judging by his expression, were not of a cheerful nature.

It wasn't until, at his own request, I dropped him off at a pub in Holland Park that I received any clue as to what they consisted of. He was standing on the pavement, saying goodbye and making an effort to sound sincere in his thanks for the expedition, when I was struck by a recollection. Rolling down the window again, I called out:

'Hang on a sec, Rodney, you've forgotten Toby's script. It's on the back seat.'

'No, it isn't.'

'It must be. I saw you put it there.'

'I know, but you didn't see me take it out again. You were upstairs, powdering your nose. I left it in the hall.'

'What on earth for?'

To give him his due, he did not request me to mind

140

my own business, although I could see it was a near thing, but said:

'I'll phone Toby and explain. Being a writer himself, I think he'll see it from my angle. I hope so, because, if not, there's damn all I can do about it.'

'Oh, I see. Well, in that case, I hope you have a lovely evening.'

'Now, don't get snooty, Tessa, for God's sake. Things are bad enough without that. I realise I've wasted everyone's time and I'm sorry, but it just can't be helped. Believe me, I'd only mess it up if I did take it on. If I'd been honest with myself, I'd have realised it all along.'

'Because you can't concentrate on anything, so long as you have Eliza's script hanging over you? Is that it?'

'That's more or less it, although hanging is the wrong word. Jostling for first place would describe it better. Even while I was with Toby and talking about the other business, my mind kept straying back to it, so I might as well face the fact now, instead of later. I'm sorry if you feel I've let you down.'

'No, it's OK, Rodney. I don't feel that at all. Good night and I really do hope you have a lovely evening.'

< 3 >

'Naturally, I wasn't going to quarrel with him over it,' I explained when describing the episode to Robin, 'but, in fact, I could have borne up quite bravely if he'd had a perfectly foul evening and been mugged on the way home.'

'That sounds rather a stiffish penalty for such a small offence, if you'll forgive me saying so.'

'Well, after all, Robin, one expects great artists and geniuses to keep chopping and changing their minds every

141

two minutes and behave like prima donnas, but— '

'I don't see why one should expect anything of the sort.'

'Well, no, perhaps not, but at least it would be excusable. Whereas for good old plodding, unimaginative Rodney suddenly to go temperamental on us is not the same thing at all. The fact is that this crusade for promoting Eliza as the great television writer of our time is becoming a morbid obsession. I suppose the truth is that he's always been more than half in love with her.'

'That sounds very penetrating and clever, but I suspect your real grouse is that you were having a whale of a time being everyone's little Mrs Fix-it and you can't tolerate opposition or any hitch in your plans.'

'Honestly, Robin, you are in a critical mood this evening. Perhaps we had better change the subject. What news on the main story? Any sign of a breakthrough yet?'

'If you refer to Eliza's death, one or two chinks have appeared in the murk, but nothing sensational.'

'Chinks are better than nothing. What light do they cast?'

'Well, you remember that Eliza spent her first night after the show in an hotel at the company's expense and thereafter she was on her own, so to speak? In fact, it turned out that she had arranged to keep the room on for an extra three nights. After which it was generally assumed that she would catch a plane back to Australia. However, it now appears that she was planning to spend another five or six weeks in London.'

'Well, that's interesting. Didn't it present any difficulties?'

'No. She had a two-way ticket, with open date for return.'

'What does surprise me is that nobody knew about it. Didn't she mention it to anyone?'

'Apparently not, or at any rate only to the airline people and there one has to say there seems to have been a degree of inefficiency. She called the office in London, giving them an outline of her plans and saying that she would call round in a day or two to make a firm booking for her return journey. Well, as you may imagine, they don't make hard and fast reservations on the strength of a telephone call, just provisional ones until the customer turns up with the ticket, which in this case never happened. The clerk, who had jotted down the name and a few other details might have been a bit quicker off the mark, but you can't altogether blame him for not coming up with the information until more than a week later. Naturally, she'd given him her married name, so he had no inkling at all that she was anyone special or celebrated and when the days went by and she didn't turn up the whole episode went out of his mind.'

'He might have made the connection when the news of her death came out.'

'Yes, he might, but you have to remember that for the average newspaper reader it didn't have quite the same impact as for you lot in the theatre. Also in the press reports all the emphasis was on her family name, you'd hardly have realised she wasn't still called Deverell. It was only by a fluke that when he was sorting the papers on his desk that he came across the details he'd written down concerning the cancelling of Mrs Jones's reservation and awaiting her instructions and some tiny bell started to ring in his head. Luckily, he decided to act on it.'

'Even so, I can't see that it makes much difference. The fact that she was planning to stay for an extra six weeks doesn't get us any nearer to finding out how she died.'

'Perhaps not, but the fact that she had kept her plans secret even from her family, so they claim, could have a very important bearing.'

'Well, yes, I suppose you're right. Someone could have found out and, being determined to prevent it, had decided that murder would be the best way. Perhaps I had better forget about swimming pools and coasters and all Toby's

143

troubles and concentrate on this new development.'

'And how would you propose to set about that?'

'Goodness knows. The object, of course, will be to find out whatever I can about this change of plans and why she didn't want anyone to know; but it's a question of where to start, isn't it?'

THIRTEEN

The answer, or at any rate a fair slice of it, was delivered on my breakfast tray the following day, via an article in the morning paper.

Turning first to the arts page, as is my custom, attention was immediately caught by the announcement that Candida's latest film had been nominated for an Oscar. To be precise, it had been nominated several times over, not merely as best film, but for best director, score and performances by both leading players.

I thought it unlikely that Candida herself would be among the final winners, for, although she was worshipped and adored by critics and discriminating film-goers, there were one or two among the nominees for best actress who were even more deeply worshipped and adored by the distributors and box-office managers of three continents. However, this presented no obstacle to telephoning to congratulate her, which I lost no time in doing, it being a case of more haste more speed.

I was aware that by ten o'clock approximately four hundred other people would feel that the moment had arrived to pick up the telephone for the same purpose, but I also happened to know that Candida, unlike most successful actresses, was an early riser. At the very worst, a telephone call at eight thirty would only disturb her while she was polishing up her lines, or someone else's life, or possibly getting through her daily stint of Schopenhauer.

At first she pretended not to understand what I was on about, proving that she was not totally dissimilar to other successful actresses in all respects.

'Haven't you seen a paper?' I asked, having explained.

'Not yet. Nana's had a bad night and I'm waiting for the doctor.'

'Oh, I am sorry, Candida. What's the matter with her?'

'Just the usual rheumaticky aches and pains, I expect, but one can't afford to take chances with people of her age.'

'Well, I won't hold you up any longer, then. Just wanted to be among the first to congratulate you.'

'My darling, you're the very first and it was sweet of you to call. Do read it out to me again.'

I started to do so, but had not got beyond the first sentence when she interrupted:

'On second thoughts, I mustn't indulge myself now, Tessa. No knowing what the old demon will get up to, if she's left alone for ten minutes and I have a better idea. If you're free about lunchtime, why not drop in for a tiny snack and a glass of wine? I shall be tied here by the leg, keeping Nana in order and Mother's spending the day with her sister, so we'll be able to have a lovely gossip. So much I want to hear.'

I told her I would be delighted and spent the next ten minutes debating how much I would allow her to hear and how much to keep to myself.

'I saw your niece the other day,' I remarked, picking an item out of the first category, when we had dealt with Nana's indisposition and the Oscar nominations.

She was wearing no make up at all on this occasion and her pale blonde hair was hanging loose, parted in the middle and pulled back behind her ears. It would have looked most unbecoming on anyone else, but had the effect of enlarging her grey-blue eyes and accentuating the delicate contours of her face.

'Rosie? Oh, at Roakes, of course. I'd forgotten for the moment that Toby lives there. What was she up to, naughty girl?'

'Nothing much. We met in the village shop.'

'Just like that?'

'No, we'd met before. Jack Pullborough invited her over one evening when he was spending the night with Toby.'

'My goodness, that girl does get around, doesn't she? I'd no idea she moved in such exalted circles.'

'The funny thing is, she seems to get on well with people on every level. Does she remind you at all of your sister, Eliza?'

'How extraordinary that you should say that!'

'You mean other people have noticed it too?'

'I don't know about that, but it's what Eliza liked to believe herself.'

'That she and Rosie were two of a kind?'

'Exactly. Personally, I could never see it, but she always made a great pet of Rosie, right from the beginning. There was over ten years' difference in their ages, but Eliza treated her more like a sister than her niece.'

I was thinking that it probably made a nice change from being a sister who was treated like a niece, but confined myself to saying:

'And the writing too. That's another thing they had in common.'

'My dear Tessa, you're full of surprises this morning. What writing?'

'You mean, you didn't know about Rosie's play? She gave it to Jack to read and he's dead keen. At least, to be honest, I don't know whether that's true, or whether he's

147

just dazzled by your illustrious name. But Eliza certainly had a lot of talent in that line, didn't she?'

'Some. Not a lot.'

'Oh, really? I got it wrong.'

'And something tells me I haven't convinced you, so I must try and explain what I mean. Otherwise you might get the idea that I was being spiteful.'

'No, I wouldn't.'

'No, well, perhaps you don't harbour such unkind thoughts, but I'll explain anyway because I believe it may even have some slight bearing on her death. Eliza, you see, always had a brilliant imagination, but absolutely no application whatever. Even as a small child of seven or eight years old, she used to make up plays for all of us to perform for our parents and their friends. Except that they weren't strictly plays at all. What usually happened was that she'd hit on some gloriously mad or comical idea and then invent a few funny lines and situations and that was about as far as it went. It was always left to Cressy or me to do the boring bits, like developing the plot and working up to a logical climax. And exactly the same sort of thing happened when she grew up and went on the stage. You may never have seen her because it only lasted for a couple of years, but I can't begin to describe how electrifying she was. The play came alive with her first entrance, but she must have been hell to work with. Even after several performances she was never word perfect and it grew worse as the run went on. After a week or two the reaction set in, she'd lose interest and she hadn't acquired enough technique to get away with it. Luckily for her, very few of the critics ever saw her when she wasn't at her peak and I think she was wise to get out when she did and move to a totally new world. She'd made it to the top, but, as you know so well, the hard part is staying there.'

This analysis matched so closely the one I had been

given by Conrad that I was beginning to feel unsure of my ground by the time she reached the end of it. Nevertheless, there was also Rodney's version to be taken into account and his, at least, had up-to-date evidence to support it, so I said:

'Well, that's how you see it and you should know, but it has also been mooted that her reason for packing it in was that she fell so madly in love with the man she married that nothing else mattered and she'd have gone to live on the moon, if he'd asked her to.'

'Oh, very true, no doubt, but one of his main attractions was that he offered total escape, with lots of new challenges and new opportunities to shine as the brightest star in the firmament. So much more thrilling than staying on and watching lesser talents leave her behind.'

'Only they might not have. If she hadn't fallen in love she might have grown up and turned herself into a real actress.'

'Well, it would be silly for us to argue about it, Tessa. You asked for my opinion and I've given it. Can't say fairer than that.'

'And you don't take to the idea that marriage and being out of the world for so long might have changed her?'

'No, nothing would do that. What makes you so interested, by the way?'

'It's just that I was wondering whether she had decided that, after all, writing was her real *métier* and had taken it up seriously and whether there could be any connection between that and her decision to stay on here for a bit longer than originally planned.'

'Oh, you've heard about that too, have you? My, my, news doesn't half travel fast.'

'Well, it won't travel any further, you may depend on that. I was told in strictest confidence and I only mention it because I was aware that you'd have heard about it long before I did.'

'Not so very long. That nice Sergeant brought us the news yesterday. As you say, she had decided to stay on for an extra few weeks. In my opinion, there is a perfectly simple, unsensational explanation, although my mother doesn't agree with me. She has convinced herself that Eliza never had any intention of going back to Conrad, once she had made the break. Luckily, I managed to head her off when I saw her on the brink of pouring it all out to the Sergeant. God knows, we're in enough trouble as it is, without providing more fodder for rumours and innuendo.'

'And what do you regard as the simple, unsensational explanation?'

'A most practical one. As you doubtless also know, one reason for her seizing this chance of a free trip to London was that she'd been having a lot of trouble with her back over the past few years. She wanted to see a specialist about it and that's exactly what she did. He's a man called Henderson, who runs a private clinic with two other doctors at Windsor and his wife is distantly related to Conrad, so nothing could have been more open and above board. Anyway, he had advised her to put off her return for a week or two and go into his clinic for treatment. Eliza, as usual, was being naughty about it, saying she couldn't possibly leave Conrad on his own for so long. We did our best to make her see how it might improve the quality of her life and it must have got through to her finally because, whatever Mother may say, I'm positive that's the one and only reason why she changed her flight.'

It was logical, up to a point, but in my opinion it left a number of loose ends. Why, for instance, since they were so concerned, had Eliza not told her family about her change of plans immediately after, if not before, arranging

150

it with the airline? More mysterious still was her neglecting to inform Alec Henderson.

However, I was in the satisfactory position of having obtained more information than I had given away, so I did not pursue the subject, allowing the conversation to drift on to the more neutral one of whether there should or should not be a memorial service for Eliza. Evadne, it appeared, was in favour, but Candida inclined to regard it as inappropriate in the circumstances. She did not enter into the controversy with any of her usual vehemence, though, and I suspected that she was already turning over ideas in her mind for her plain and simple dress, if not acceptance speech, at the dinner for the Oscar awards.

FOURTEEN

'The news is not all bad,' Toby announced on the telephone the next morning.

'Put it another way. What is good about it?'

'Brian has left home.'

'Yes, I do call that fairly good. Did he have a tiff with his young lady?'

'I rather doubt it. She did not strike me as one to whom tiffs would come naturally. According to Mrs Parkes, things were getting rather hot for him here and he felt it was time to move elsewhere and lie low for a bit.'

'More burglaries?'

'So they say.'

'Not caught in the act, by any chance?'

'No and, so far as I know, they have not been reported to the police either.'

'Why do you suppose that is?'

'I think it must be on account of the name, you know. Everyone has a pretty good idea about who the culprit is, but they feel reluctant to stir up trouble for such an influential family as those Deverells. How sensible of Rosie not to marry any of her suitors. She is on much firmer ground as a spinster.'

'Well, as to that, I think she may be about to change course with the current one. However, that's part of a new theory which is beginning to take shape at the moment. I'll let you know how it works out, if you like.'

'I am sure you will,' he replied, 'whether I do or not.'

It was a great day for family togetherness and I had scarcely dropped the telephone back on its hook when it rang again. This time it was Ellen and she began, unusually for her, with a complaint:

'I really do think, Tessa, that it's about time you got yourself a separate telephone line. I can't see why Robin should mind and people do get so fussed when they spend hours searching through the telephone book, sometimes ringing up all sorts of other Crichtons, before they discover that you're hidden away under Price.'

'It can be inconvenient,' I admitted. 'I had an example of it recently, but it has its advantages too. All my friends know exactly how to find me, whereas to the double glaziers and that lot I am virtually incommunicado. On the whole, I prefer things to remain as they are. Who's been fussing now?'

'You'll never guess. It was Conrad.'

'No, I wouldn't have guessed.'

'And that's another thing, Tessa. You would have it that his only interest in you was as someone he could gabble away to, with no strings attached, but it doesn't sound like that to me. He sounded as though he had something really urgent to say to you.'

'Well, if he has, it's not a declaration of undying love, I can assure you. He was very chatty over lunch, but he never asked me a single question about myself. It was more like a conversation with someone on a train.'

'Oh well, perhaps he just wanted to say goodbye.'

'You mean he's leaving us?'

'At the end of the week, apparently. Venetia can't wait to wave goodbye. That is, if she has the strength left to

153

raise an arm. She finds him rather tempestuous after stolid old Alec.'

'Personally, if I had to choose between them, I'd prefer Conrad any old day. That Alec is not only stolid, he's terribly smug and disapproving with it.'

'That's true. And he certainly disapproved of Eliza, for one.'

'How do you know?'

'Venetia told me. She tried every trick in her book to prise something out of him on that subject, you may be sure, but the closest he ever got to an indiscretion was when he heard that Eliza had committed suicide. He said he wasn't at all surprised because she was a very wayward and headstrong young woman.'

'Yes, I can just hear him saying it. Did you give Conrad my number, by the way?'

'Had to, didn't I? He was going to try and ring you this morning.'

'He'll have to look sharp, then. I'm going out in a minute and after that he'll be entirely at Mrs Cheeseman's mercy.'

There were no messages on the pad when I arrived home that evening, however, so either he had lost the urge to say goodbye, or else had been foiled in the attempt. The fact that there wasn't one from Robin either, saying that he would be back late, was even better news and as soon as he was sitting comfortably, with a drink at his side, I introduced the subject of what had by then become known as the Deverell case.

'I gather Conrad is now allowed to leave the country,' I began.

'It's not really a question of allowing, is it? There's no pretext for holding him here or confiscating his passport.'

'I am rather surprised that he should want to go. I

154

would have expected him to stick it out to the end.'

'Perhaps he would have preferred to, but had no choice. He was sent for out of the blue and presumably had to leave his house and travel to the other side of the world at a few hours' notice. All sorts of mayhem may have been piling up for him while he's been away.'

'I suppose that was quite genuine, was it? There couldn't have been any trick about it?'

'How do you mean? He arrived here in not much over forty-eight hours, which is pretty prompt in the circumstances.'

'In fact, I was wondering, given the circumstances, if it had been a shade too prompt?'

'Oh, I see. The theory being that he was so confident the event would take place, having organised it himself by remote control, that when the message came he was all packed up and ready to leave, with tickets and passport in his coat pocket. Is that it? If so, I'm afraid it wouldn't count against him in a court of law.'

'I realise that, I was just curious to know how he managed to get here so quickly. I'd been under the impression that this island of his was completely out of contact with the rest of the world.'

'Yes, I was curious myself, so I did a little checking up. It turns out to be on the southern fringes of a group of islands, of which the largest and nearest to the twentieth century has a port, telephone system and airstrip. It also has a part-time consul, a local businessman, who works for an Australian firm. He is provided with a launch, which is used for taking monthly deliveries of mail and newspapers to the outer islands, together with certain basic provisions and medical supplies. It can also be used in emergencies for unscheduled trips and this was the means whereby Conrad learnt of his wife's death and was able to get out and be on a flight to Perth within twenty-four hours. Satisfied?'

155

'Absolutely, thank you, Robin, and I can tell from the brisk way you reel it all off that his movements thereafter have been just as thoroughly checked.'

'They have, as a matter of fact, although it was a largely superfluous exercise. On arriving at Perth, he found there was no plane to London until the following day, but he managed to get a seat on a flight bound for New York, with a stopover in Zurich. There he switched to a London flight, which got him into Heathrow five or six hours later. He had cabled his arrival time and was met as he came off the plane by someone from the Yard, who accompanied him to the hotel, where he spent the first night of his stay. So, you see, there's no way at all whereby he could have reached this country one minute earlier than he did.'

'Yes, I do see. I'd been playing with the idea that he might have worked some trick with two passports, but obviously that's out and on the whole I'm glad to have got it cleared up. Despite all your cautionary tales, I never could see him as a murderer and neither could Ellen.'

'And now, like everyone else, you're back to the beginning again?'

'Is that really how it stands? No progress at all?'

'Not so far as I've heard. On the face of it, it looked like murder or manslaughter, but no shadow of motive and no evidence at all has been found to support it, so opinion was veering round to suicide again. That, of course, got the thumbs down when it came out that she was planning to extend her stay for an extra five or six weeks. It seems to leave accidental death as the only acceptable verdict.'

'Although I suppose you could argue that her change of plan does re-open the possibility of murder by a jot or two?'

'Could you? How?'

'Well, I know it sounds far fetched, but suppose someone had overheard her call to the airline and then either

156

he, or someone else he'd passed the news on to, wasn't best pleased about it?'

'Hardly a motive for murder, would you say?'

'Well, she had a strong will, you know, and she was famous for getting her own way. And very talented too, don't forget. Some people might have been quite happy to wave goodbye to her eight years ago and not best pleased by the prospect of her staying on. They're very ruthless, those Deverells.'

'They would need to be, Tess. And it was only a postponement. She couldn't have created any serious havoc for them in six weeks.'

'Oh, that could have been just a trial period she had allotted herself. If things had worked out for her, she could have torn up her air ticket and stayed on. If not, nothing lost and she could bow out without losing face. And no one could deny that they're the only ones who had all the opportunities they needed for switching the pills.'

'It could be said that I have endless opportunities for switching yours, but it doesn't follow that I would.'

'That's good, and perhaps you'll be even less tempted to when I tell you that I have another string to my bow.'

'Better or worse than the last one?'

'Both, possibly. That's what I have to try and find out. The motive, if it does exist, would be a real corker. Opportunity is more tricky because, as we've said, absolutely anyone could have gone up to her room after she came back to the hotel that evening, without bothering to have themselves announced at the desk. Just a tap on the bedroom door and she'd have opened up and let them in, you may be sure.'

'Just to tie things up, I should perhaps point out that the only one who couldn't have done that was Conrad. However, I suppose you have your own ideas as to who it might have been. In which case, I can only warn you not

157

to make yourself too unpopular by going around asking loaded questions.'

'No, I won't. All I'm hoping for is a friendly chat with one or two people and I think it might be best to start with Rosie.'

'What's Rosie got to do with it?'

'I'm not sure, but there's growing evidence to suggest that she knew a lot more about what went on in her Aunt Eliza's life than most people did and the fact that she was out and about that evening, in semi-disguise, must have some significance. According to Nana, she was looking very smart and well turned out, for once.'

'Got herself up to kill, in other words?'

'Well no, I wouldn't go as far as that, but certainly enough to make herself unrecognisable to anyone whose only previous sight of her had been on television for "Birthday Tribute".'

As it happened, this was not the whole truth either, but I had been chasing so many hares by this time that, rather than confuse the issue still further, I had decided to leave it in as the curtain line for Act Two. Time enough to start getting to grips with the lurking suspicion that someone with a sharp eye, who happened to have a special interest in Eliza, might not have been taken in for a moment by Rosie's semi-disguise.

By the time the intermission was over, which is to say by ten o'clock the following morning, I had decided to enlarge the field for speculation by bringing on a new character for the opening of Act Three.

FIFTEEN

< 1 >

Joan Manders-Hobson and I had been at school together for a brief period and during one summer had been finalists in the singles tennis competition and also joint winners of the divinity prize, although this had less to do with our interest in the subject than our love for the young curate, who had been coming one evening a week throughout that term to give the confirmation classes.

Soon afterwards, my interest in spiritual matters having waned and my affections been transferred to a pop singer, I had left that school under a small cloud, but Joan had gone from strength to strength. In her last year she had been head girl, as well as captain of lacrosse and had subsequently gone to Oxford, where she almost certainly got an honours degree, if not two.

Our friendship, naturally, had gone into decline during that period, but it had revived and flourished as never before when we found ourselves caught up in the same production and surrounded on all sides by fearful outsiders who hadn't been at school with us. It was no great surprise, either, to find that, although she had fallen out of love with the curate at the age of sixteen, she could still reel off details of his later career, the name of his wife, number of children and the parish in London where he was now the incumbent. Such thorough and meticulous attention to inessentials, in addition to the other qualifications, had inevitably turned her into one of the most highly valued research workers in the business.

As it happened, I had once or twice enlisted these talents to assist in some private research of my own and so, considering this to be the logical move in the current stalemate, I invited her to meet me for lunch at a restaurant round the corner from her office and had spent the first few minutes before getting down to business in complimenting her on her appearance. No artifice was needed for this, for she was tall, straight and slim, attributes which had given her the edge on the lacrosse field, with deep-set eyes, a clear complexion and teeth that were just, but only just irregular enough to prove that they were not capped. She was also on that day, as on every other, immaculately coiffed, dressed and made up.

'I can give you a certain amount of information without any fishing around at all,' she replied, in answer to my first question.

'Why's that? Have you seen him lately?'

'Not for weeks, but you know how it is? The word gets around even when the subject doesn't.'

'And what is the word?'

'That he was due for the chop. That last series that he and Derek worked on together, I don't suppose you saw it, all about working men's clubs, was just not on. Excessively dreary and *déjà vu* and an absolute pill as far as the ratings went.'

Déjà vu was the favourite expression in the business at that time and I had known I could rely on Joan to bring it out in the first ten minutes.

'Yes, I did hear terrible tales,' I admitted, 'but I thought

160

he had lived it down and was now working on some police serial?'

'Oh, my dear Tessa, you're miles out of date. That was all washed up long ago.'

'What went wrong there?'

'Oh, usual, I suppose. Presumably, what he was turning out was so unbelievably dull and pedestrian that no one in his right mind could ever imagine it taking off. Poor Rodney, he's competent enough, in his way, but the truth is that he hasn't bothered to keep pace with the new trends and styles. He just goes plodding on in the same groove he dug for himself six or eight years ago. It's all so— '

Cutting in before she could pass the dreaded verdict of *déjà vu* yet again, I said, 'But listen, Joan, I got the impression from the way you spoke that the crisis had been averted. Did you mean that, despite everything, he's now back in favour?'

'Edging his way towards it, I would say. He's come up with an original script, eight episodes, which he must have been beavering away at for months. I haven't read any of them myself, but I know someone who has and he's madly impressed. Goes around saying old Rodney's had a new lease of life and will surprise us all yet.'

'A new lease of life is exactly what he has had.'

'Oh yes? Where from?'

'Well, for heaven's sake, Joan, if you know this much, you must know the lot. Those scripts were not his own unaided work, you know. They were the brain child of Eliza Deverell, who finished work on them just before she died.'

'Yes, I heard all about that. Rodney is the first to say that the original idea was hers and that she contributed some brilliant dialogue. He's very insistent about her name being on the credits too. Some people consider that very generous of him.'

161

'That's one way of looking at it.'

'Personally, I regard it as rather a shrewd move on his part.'

'And that's another. Why do you say so?'

'Well, you only have to remember the weight that name carries, don't you? People might not have been in such a hurry to read it, in the first place, without the Deverell tag, and, given what's happened during the past couple of weeks, it's worth its weight in gold in advance publicity.'

'You think it might have worked out differently if Eliza had still been alive?'

'Oh, heavens, how the hell would I know? That's not my department. For all I know, she might not have wanted her name anywhere near it, or on the other hand, she might have stuck out for sole writer's credit.'

'Yes, I suppose she might.'

'Since we'll never know, it hardly seems worth worrying about. The sensible thing is to make the best of what's on offer and this time it seems to be pretty good.'

'OK, no need to french polish it, as my father-in-law would say.'

'Your father-in-law has an inexhaustible fund of colourful sayings. I sometimes wonder if you invented him.'

'No, I didn't and, just as a matter of interest, Joan, how did your lot manage to get in touch with Eliza in the first place?'

'No problem. We simply applied to Candida, as we did for most of our contacts in the initial stages, and she told us exactly how to go about it. As you'll recall, it was always part of the scheduled programme to show a film clip of Eliza. We have a reciprocal arrangement with a company in Sydney, who handled all that side of it for us. It was only after she arrived there that we telephoned to ask how she'd feel about coming over, in person.'

'And she jumped at it, I suppose?'

'Not exactly. In fact, she was inclined to be hesitant at first. Said she'd have to talk it over with her husband before committing herself. Luckily, he'd come over to Sydney with her, so she was able to call us back the next day and say it was on. So there's another subject for speculation, if you need one.'

'Where?'

'Whether she honestly believed he might raise objections, or whether she was dubious herself and he talked her round.'

'I hardly see him making that sort of sacrifice on behalf of his hated mother-in-law.'

'Unless it wasn't a sacrifice at all and he rather welcomed the chance to get shot of Eliza for a week or so.'

'Honestly, Joan, I never thought I'd live to say this, but I begin to wonder if you've missed your vocation. Perhaps you ought to have been a fiction writer yourself.'

'Thanks for the warning and, since it's nearly two, I'd better get back to my last. It's been fun seeing you, Tessa. We must do this more often. My treat next time, don't forget.'

'Well, as to that,' I said, 'it strikes me that I gained much more from this one than you did. You've been most helpful.'

'Oh, come on, now, don't pretend you've learnt anything you didn't already know or couldn't have guessed.'

'Maybe not, but what you have done is to put it all into the right order for me, cutting out the inessentials and ending up with a logical pattern. That's my idea of a treat.'

< 2 >

'Any chance of talking to the master?' I asked Mrs Parkes.

'I can but ask. He's only upstairs, but he's bound to want to know what it's about.'

'To tell you the truth, it's pretty stifling in London just now and I was wondering about the current situation regarding the swimming pool.'

'I can tell you that myself, without moving from this spot. They've cleaned it out and filled it up again and everything's in working order.'

'Three cheers, but was it a wise move? You haven't been invaded as a result?'

'No, that Rosie's been up here the last two afternoons, but she doesn't come in the house and it looks like she's on her best behaviour, now she's on her own. Leaves the baby under a tree while she has her swim, spends a few minutes chatting to Mr Crichton, if he happens to be down there and then off she goes in that ramshackle old car of hers. You couldn't call it a nuisance, really.'

'And Brian's gone for good, has he?'

'Looks like it.'

'He doesn't seem to have put up much of a fight. Was it really because things were getting too hot for him, or was there some other reason for his leaving?'

'A bit of both, I shouldn't wonder.'

'Both what?'

'Well, it's like this, you see. There have been one or two things gone missing from people's houses and that, but nothing of much value and some of them have been returned. So it was a nuisance more than anything and most people took the view that he was a bit touched and that it wasn't a matter for the police so much as one of those psychiatrists. But Parkes and I wondered if his young lady had seen the red light and told him to mend his ways, or else get on his bike, and it was more likely she'd have been the one putting the things back.'

'All the same, I wouldn't have expected him to cave in so easily. What's the other bit?'

'That was my friend, Mrs Daly's idea. We were talking

164

about it when she dropped in to return a cake tin I'd lent her and she said there might be some item he'd pinched and then found some shady jeweller to take it off his hands and that someone, naming no names, was on to it and had threatened to prosecute.'

'Like if this someone's wife had lost a valuable ring, for instance?'

'Or making out she had, even if it wasn't true, would do just as well. Brian would find it hard work proving it wasn't him that had taken it.'

I told her that I saw exactly what she meant and also that I would be down the following afternoon, unless she were to let me know that it would not be convenient.

When I had rung off it struck me that Robin, who had sometimes accused me of possessing a devious mind, could count himself lucky not to be married to Mrs Daly.

'I know how much you dislike talking shop,' I told him a few hours later, 'but I'd like to try you out on motives.'

'If you must. For murder, I suppose?'

'That's right, as Rosie would say. You told me once that about fifty per cent of them in this country are committed in the home. True?'

'Must be, if I said it.'

'In other words, people who have once loved someone can kill him or her as easily as not?'

'I'm sure I didn't go as far as that, but it does happen. They can also kill someone they still love.'

'Jealousy, you mean?'

'That's right.'

'Now, don't you start! It can so easily become a habit and it wouldn't sound right on you. Well, at least that would bear out Evadne's theory about Conrad, although she doesn't seem to have much factual evidence to back it up. Besides, I find it hard to believe that the *crime passionnel* is a very popular pastime among the northern races. What would you say is the most common motive for these domestic murders, apart from drunken brawls?'

'Personal gain.'

'For money, in other words?'

'Not necessarily, although that, as you would put it, is probably the most popular incentive; but there's another side to it, as well. That tiresome, demanding old relative upstairs, hanging on to life, can become quite a powerful motive, with or without money thrown in. What is all this leading up to, by the way?'

'I was really trying to find out whether there were any precedents for someone committing a murder for gain, even though, in some curious, twisted way, he still loved the victim?'

'Plenty, I should say. After all, few of us are totally devoid of filial affection. So, faced with that conflict, what better than to rationalise their actions with comforting words about putting an end to Mum's or Granny's suffering? In some cases, it may well be genuine. However— '

'What?'

'Is it relevant here? Something tells me it's not the demise of some senile relative which concerns you at the moment. In which case, I haven't been much help, have I?'

'Yes, you have because talking about it has made me see something which hadn't occurred to me before.'

'What could that be, I wonder?'

'It was you saying that to be entirely devoid of filial affection would be unnatural, but of course the same rule wouldn't apply to falling out of love with someone you'd once been potty about. Furthermore, it's a condition which you have to take people's word for. If Mr Brown went about explaining to everyone that he adored his mother, they'd think he was off his head, but if he should tell you that he's dotty about someone called Daisy Smith, who happens to be married to Mr Smith, you'd have no reason to disbelieve him.'

'And when Daisy was found strangled by an unknown hand Mr Brown would be the last one they'd suspect?'

'Well, it's the beginnings of a theory, don't you agree?'

'I suppose so. Almost worthy of Mrs Daly, in fact, but I strongly advise you not to set about trying to prove it. Your Mr Brown sounds rather an undesirable character, who might not take kindly to an outsider meddling in his affairs.'

'Although, to be fair, it could just be a question of proving the theory to be false and crossing his name off the list. The real snag, though, is that I can't quite see what form the meddling could take. Presumably, if I were to ask him outright, it could get me into trouble, but I can't at the moment see any way of going about it without him realising what I was up to.'

'It could also be the signal for him to start running around, telling his friends that he's madly in love with you.'

'Yes, it's a tricky one and no mistake. Perhaps I should drop that theory, for the time being and concentrate on Rosie.'

'You're always saying that, it's becoming your theme song, but you never seem to get beyond the first line of the lyric.'

'I know, but she's a hard one to crack too, always shying away from the direct answer, not backwards, but sideways. I expect she was born under the sign of Cancer. All the same, I think it's worth another shot. I've always believed that she knows a damn sight more than she's let on. At one point I thought blackmail might be her game, but I've gone off that idea since she and Brian split up. On the other hand, she might be protecting someone, or maybe just sitting back and enjoying the spectacle of the police being totally baffled, Lord Peter. Whatever it is, I mean to have one more go at her when I'm at Roakes tomorrow.'

SIXTEEN

An unearthly silence had settled over the house and garden, which was partially accounted for by a note on the hall table, which read as follows:

'Have put tea things out in kitchen for you and Mr Crichton, so as you can make your own when you're ready. Biscuits and cakes in the tins. Mr Crichton lunching in Oxford, said he'd be back about five.'

He was better than her word, however, and staggered in fifteen minutes ahead of schedule and clutching two stout parcels from a well-known bookshop.

'You look very grand,' I told him, 'in your natty gent's suiting.'

'I come from a grand place,' he replied, 'and shall now go upstairs and change into something more suited to my present surroundings. As I understand you are here to take a dip in the pool, you will doubtless wish to do the same.'

'That had been my intention, but I am now toying with the idea of taking a cup of tea and a biscuit or two first.'

'Is that wise? I have heard tell that it is a mistake to swim on a full stomach.'

'Yes, I've heard it tell too and, come to think of it, it may account for the corpse which is floating on top of your pool.'

'What are you talking about, Tessa?'

'I noticed it as soon as I arrived, although I didn't have the nerve to go very close. She's lying on her back, hair streaming out behind. Not so many clothes, but otherwise Millais's Ophelia to the life, or rather death. There's an inert bundle lying on the grass, which may also conceal a corpse, for all I know. Ought you to do something about it?'

'There is nothing either of us can do. She is engaged in her transcendental meditation. I discovered too late in the day that herein lies the principal attraction of our swimming pool. Apparently, floating on still water provides the ideal conditions for loosening the ties with the material world, setting the spirit free to soar uncluttered into the timeless limbo of nothingness, or words to that effect, and it may go on for hours. Time, as we know it, has no meaning when the soul is on the move.'

'It sounds rather unsociable and I am not sure that I feel like plunging in and having to make a detour each time, as I splash up and down. Can nothing be done to bring her out of this trance?'

'Well, you could try giving the bundle a sharp tap with the toe of your shoe, so that it wakes up and starts to bellow. Parkes has found this dodge quite effective. Or you could try calling out "Anyone for tea?" That would probably do the trick just as well and would certainly show a more charitable attitude. I shall leave you to make up your own mind while I go and change.'

The biscuits and cakes were out of their tins and the kettle on the boil by the time he came down again.

'I did as you suggested,' I told him, 'and it worked like a charm. She will join us in a few minutes. The curious thing is, you know, Toby, that at one time Robin and I both had the idea that you had fallen for Rosie, but, if so,

169

you appear to have become disenchanted rather smartly.'

'Oh, she's not a bad girl,' he replied. 'We get on tolerably well, now that we have both made our positions clear.'

'I see. And what positions would those be?'

'Well, it was a wrench, in a way, because it's true that I find her not altogether devoid of charm, but I soon realised that there was only room for one playwright in my life.'

'I expect it was a wise decision. What was Rosie's position?'

'She signified in her oblique way that she did not care much for the younger man and more often than not only took up with one because he seemed so helpless and dependent. However, if she were ever to form an ongoing and meaningful relationship, it would have to be with someone experienced and mature. That brought me up sharp, I can tell you. A little flirtation over the martini glasses on the fine summer evenings is all very well, but the role of father figure, kissing away the tears of his child bride is not one which I feel myself to be cut out for.'

'Then perhaps you should count yourself lucky that your understudy was waiting in the wings. She might not have let you off so easily, if it had not been for him.'

'Oh well, as to that, it would be a mistake to place too much reliance on Mrs Parkes's opinions. She is apt to see life through purple tinted glasses, particularly those aspects of it which touch on marital infidelity. Ah, there you are, Rosie! Come and join us. Tessa and I were just talking about you.'

She gave no sign of either surprise or curiosity on learning this, evidently finding it a most natural thing for us to be doing. Instead, she took a cup with one hand and scooped up a slice of cake with the other, remarking that she was ravenous and causing Ned to flop back on her knees and let out a howl of rage.

'Oh, sorry, sorry,' she said, re-arranging him in a sitting position and jogging her legs up and down, which at least had the effect of taking too much of his breath away to leave him enough to scream with. Sensing, perhaps, that it might only be a temporary reprieve, Toby refilled his cup and announced that he would take it upstairs and have a browse through his new books.

'Does a stint of meditation always work up an appetite?' I asked when he had gone and Rosie had started weighing into the biscuits.

'Quite often, yes.'

'I can't think how you manage to stay so thin. I'd have expected all that sitting about and letting the mind wander, in between hearty meals, to be so bad for the figure.'

'No, you don't understand, Tessa. It's not a bit like that. Real, deep meditation uses up more calories than running in a marathon. It's been proved by lots of people. I'll explain it all to you properly one day, if you're interested.'

Wishing to avoid the direct lie, I said:

'How did you learn so much about it? You've been to India?'

'That's right. Me and a friend went together, overland through Bulgaria and Turkey and we spent about six weeks in an ashram in southern India. We had planned to go on to China and try and get into Tibet, but my friend got dysentery and he had to fly home and it was a bit complicated after that. Lots of red tape and restrictions and stuff, you know, about women travelling on their own in those parts.'

'I can imagine. So what did you do? Give it up and come home yourself?'

'No, I stayed with someone I knew in Bangkok for a bit and then I went on to Australia and New Zealand. When I got as far as that, I thought I might as well go back via California and spend a few weeks in LA, where one of my

171

aunts was making a film, but just about then I discovered I was pregnant and that would have been a restriction too, so I packed it in and came back here.'

'What a shame! Still, it was good while it lasted, I expect and, at least, you can say that it changed your life in a couple of ways.'

'Which ways?'

'Well, your meditation, for one, which seems to be important to you, and you've also got Ned now, don't forget.'

'Oh no, I won't forget Ned,' Rosie said and burst into laughter. There was something so joyous and infectious in it that I found myself joining in, but it was not just parrot laughter on my part. There had been something about the way she looked down at the baby and ruffled his hair when I mentioned him which gave rise to amusement, as well as a touch of elation.

The remnants of both must still have been hanging around when I arrived back at Beacon Square because Robin, who for once had arrived home ahead of me, asked whether he should pour me a drink, or whether I had stopped off for a couple on the way.

'Absolutely not,' I told him, 'sober as a judge.'

'Ah well, it must have been the exercise which has given you this aura of well being.'

'Not that, either. In fact, I'd left it so late that it didn't seem worth while getting my hair wet. If you want the truth, the aura comes from the belief that I am on my way to winning my bet.'

It took a moment or two to get the memory jogged and then he said:

'You mean you have solved that little mystery of Eliza's death?'

'Perhaps not quite,' I admitted. 'There are still a few

172

loose ends to be tied up here and there and something I need to confirm about Eliza, but it's about time I paid another courtesy call on Evadne, anyway and, if that doesn't do it, Ellen may be able to get what I need from Venetia. None of it should take long, though, and, if I'm on the right track at last, I foresee no difficulty in meeting the deadline.'

SEVENTEEN

'Poor old Rodney!' I remarked more or less at random during our celebration dinner, which took place in a gourmet's paradise within a stone's throw of the Charing Cross Road.

We had invited Toby to join us and he had accepted on one condition. In order to prevent any tedious wrangling on the subject between Robin and me, he would pay the bill.

'I can't help feeling sorry for him,' I added, 'and I still have a sneaking hope that he'll get away with it.'

They both looked rather shocked by this and Toby said:

'Oh, come now, that's going a bit far, surely? I mean, after all, plagiarism— '

'Yes, I know, Toby, but the fact is that it wasn't exactly plagiarism, was it? It was the other way round and I can't see it as such a venal crime. He'd had it rough for so long and I suppose, like most of us, he blamed it on bad luck, rather than his own shortcomings. He'd convinced himself that he'd soon be back on top again, if only his luck would change and Eliza was to be the one to do it. Still, I suppose he should count himself lucky that he wasn't accused of anything worse.'

Toby looked sceptical, as though unwilling to believe there could be anything worse, but Robin said:

'Yes, you were all set to pin the murder on him not so long ago, weren't you?'

'I must admit I was and I'd worked out such a beautiful motive for him that I was quite sorry to see it go. It was only during my last talk with Rosie that everything began to fall into place and I saw who the real murderer must have been.'

'By such threads do our lives hang,' Toby remarked, and Robin said:

'You call it beautiful, but I was never all that impressed. The idea of someone committing a murder, in order to pinch a script and pass it off as his own work struck me as pretty incredible, even in the insane world you two inhabit. Furthermore, as I recall, he didn't claim it as his own work. He never stopped prattling on about how Eliza had done the creative part and he was just there to edit and re-shape it for her.'

'You're right, of course, and that's what made it so fascinating, because the one point on which Conrad and his hated in-laws were in complete agreement was that Eliza wouldn't have been capable of such a thing. She was brimming over with imaginative ideas, but she never bothered to develop them. As soon as that kind of chore was needed she handed it over to someone else and moved on to pastures new. Candida said, and I believe her, that it was why she gave up the stage when she looked all set for stardom. First-night ovations were just the ticket, but turning up at the theatre on time for eight performances a week was quite another thing. Naturally, Rodney meant to wring every drop he could from her name, to get the project off the ground and also to use her brilliant flashes of inspiration wherever possible, but by the end of it you can be sure that he'd have done the hard slog himself.'

'Well, as you know,' Robin replied, 'I am completely at a loss here, but wouldn't everybody who mattered have

175

known perfectly well that he couldn't have pulled it off by himself?'

'They might have been sceptical, but how could they prove anything? That's what gave me the idea that he became so obsessed with this scheme of using Eliza's script to claw his way back to the top that he finally killed her, in order to get sole possession of it. You may think that no sane man could have contemplated such a thing, but I am not sure that Rodney is always entirely sane these days and the interesting part of it is that the minute she was dead he began to change his tune. Only a day or two later he was telling me how someone had discovered a really disastrous flaw in the last episode, which Eliza had sent to him by special messenger a few hours before her death and how this was going to mean re-vamping all the previous episodes, a job which only he could do. Well, just suppose he had inserted this deliberate mistake, plus a few others too, you can see how convenient it would be if Eliza were no longer alive to tell her side of the tale? Oh yes, it was a nice theory and I was sorry to discard it. You may sympathise more when I tell you that it also included an explanation for Rodney's ambivalent attitude towards Rosie.'

'That doesn't require explanation,' Toby said. 'A good many people have an ambivalent attitude to Rosie and I am one of them.'

'I think we realised that,' Robin told him, 'but she does seem to turn up in everyone's life sooner or later, although I am at a loss to understand what part she could have played in your precious theory about Rodney. Are you going to finish your oysters, or aren't you? The waiter has been hovering for about five minutes.'

'You take two each, then and I'll deal with the last one. It is not easy to talk and eat oysters at the same time.'

'The reason why she turns up everywhere,' I said, as we waited for the next course, 'is that she was the key figure and the one who opened every door, including a few which could just as well have remained closed. What happened to lead me off course in Rodney's case was that when we passed her on the road the other day he almost certainly didn't recognise her and appeared perfectly indifferent when I explained who she was, neither trying to change the subject, nor get me to expand on it.'

'Was there any reason why he should have recognised her? She wasn't at the party for the "Birthday Tribute", if you remember?'

'No, but the sequel to my tale is that when he got a really close-up view of her that day, talking to me in the village shop, his reaction was most peculiar. He knew exactly who she was by then and there was no reason why he shouldn't have joined us, as he'd obviously intended to do before he got within close range. At that point, he first stopped in his tracks, then backed away and finally bolted out of the shop. Unfortunately for him, when I came out myself Rosie was still tagging along, so he turned his back on us and pretended to be reading the names on the War Memorial.'

'And how did you account for that?'

'Simply that the boot had changed feet and he was afraid she might recognise him.'

'Well, I must be obtuse', Toby said, 'because I'm still in the dark.'

'It hinged on something old Nana had told me. She said that one evening, she couldn't remember exactly which, but it was after the television show and before Eliza died, Rosie had left Ned with her before she went out on the town. She didn't come back to collect him until several hours later and furthermore, to use Nana's own words, she was dressed up to the nines, high-heeled shoes and

177

hair all smarmed down. In other words, unrecognisable from a distance. So my theory was based on the idea that one who did come close, but not quite close enough, was Rodney and that the time and place of this near encounter was somewhere in the vicinity of Eliza's hotel room, just before or just after she took the overdose. So that it was not until he was observing her while she talked to me that recognition dawned and he got away as fast as he could and then kept his back to her when we joined him. Now that you've heard it, you must admit that it was a neat theory and almost the best part was that it also accounted for Rodney's immediate decision to turn down the offer to adapt Toby's script. Until then he'd been quite keen to do it, but as soon as we were safely on our way to London he confessed that he'd changed his mind and left it behind. Well, everyone knows that Toby won't stir from his own hearth, if it can be avoided, least of all to go to London, so all script conferences while work was in progress would have to have been conducted at Roakes. And Roakes, so long as it contained Rosie, was a no-go area. A neat conclusion, you have to agree.'

'Oh, indeed!' Toby said, 'but since it proved to be a false one, did you ever discover the true explanation?'

'I found an alternative and, as usual, Rosie's at the root of it. It was simply that when he saw her clearly and heard her speak she reminded him so forcibly of Eliza. No, honestly, she reminded me and a great many other people of Eliza, but the difference in Rodney's case was that Eliza represented something special and unique for him. I'd always believed him to be half in love with her, but there was more to it than that. She was a budding star when they met, all set for the brightest of lights, whereas he was just an unknown ASM, without charm or talent and of no account to anyone. Nevertheless, it was he she chose as a companion to go jaunting off to movies and galleries with.

I suspect now that this was due to a flaw in her character which made her choose always to shine as the single star, rather than as part of a galaxy, but the fact remains that to Rodney, in those days, she must have been the sun and the moon as well and I don't think he ever quite got over it. Rosie, for all her superficial resemblance, must have seemed like a travesty of the real thing and I can well believe that he wouldn't ever have wanted to set eyes on her again.'

There was a longish pause here, as the lobster armoricain made its appearance, this being one of those restaurants where you ate anything except fish at your peril and the usual fuss went on about opening and tasting the wine.

'Well, now,' Toby said, when all had been concluded to his satisfaction, 'you have made a fair job of unmasking the innocent parties and then masking them up again, but you seem strangely reluctant to tell us what led you to the guilty one.'

'Naturally.'

'Why naturally?'

'Because it means admitting that Evadne was right and that I gravely underestimated her. Not that she got any of the details right, I should add, far less the motive, but my mistake was in throwing the baby out with the bath water and not allowing for the fact that, although her reasoning was based on prejudice, her instinct was sound.'

'Yes, we know all about that and how chastening it must be, but what fascinates me is how Conrad managed to be in two places at the same time. In other words, how he managed to murder his wife in a London hotel at least two days before he arrived here. I do realise that Robin has heard the explanation already, but I am sure he will bear with me for five minutes if you nip through it again.'

'It will hardly take so long. There was no difficulty about it because he had an accomplice.'

'I still don't see what help that would have been, seeing that he is the one who is known to have switched the pills.'

'But there was a time switch as well, you see. Rosie sent him the telegram announcing the sad news forty-eight hours before the event took place.'

'Well, now, that really was worth waiting for. However did she manage it?'

'Conrad had arranged everything in advance and it worked like a dream. When the second telegram arrived, the *bona fide* one that is, the honorary consul simply assumed it was a confirmation of the first and he certainly wouldn't have troubled to make the trip out to the island with it, even if he hadn't known that Conrad was already on the first leg of his journey by then.'

'But surely there still remained the matter of arriving in this country on the right day and they tell me that he not only did so, but was greeted by a posse from Scotland Yard as he stepped off the plane.'

'As it happens, Toby, it wasn't much of a problem. In the first place, for what appeared to be perfectly practical reasons, he broke his journey and changed planes at Zurich. In the second, he'd formerly been employed by a UN agency and still did consultancy jobs for them, from time to time, which means that he'd automatically have held a United Nations passport, in addition to his national one. So you can see how dead simple it would have been to travel as far as Europe on one, over to London and back again on the other and finally to London again on the first one.'

'Oh yes, very crafty! And so how did he pass the time on that first visit? Surely not by marching into Eliza's hotel room and saying: "Ah, good evening! I just popped over to make sure you're taking your pills"?'

'No, he marched in all right, but there was no need to

say anything at all because she wasn't there. She went out to dinner that night and by the time she returned he had finished his work and gone. She was dining with Rosie, who, as you know, had always been her pet and protégée. Hence Rosie's disguise. There was small chance of her being recognised, because she didn't move in the same circles as the rest of the family, but she'd been instructed not to take unnecessary risks. It's one more example of the thoroughness with which Conrad masterminded the whole operation.'

'I find myself almost disliking him for it,' Toby said.

'It is normal for people to dislike murderers when they have been exposed as such,' Robin told him. 'The trouble comes from many of them being so likeable before the event. Isn't that so, Tessa?'

'I have to agree that in this case it is. I relied on my intuition and it let me down with a thump. My only excuse is that Ellen's intuition passed on the same message and we all know that she is not given to instant favourable judgements. All the same,' I added hurriedly, lest the last remark might tempt Toby to unleash a few unfavourable comments about Jeremy, 'there were a couple of give-aways during my lunch session with Conrad, which might have shown me how the land lay, if I'd been more detached. It was Evadne's fault, really, even more than Ellen's. She was so vitriolic about him that I was naturally on his side even before we met.'

'What did he give away when you had lunch with him?' Robin asked, sounding faintly as though he suspected it of being a diamond bracelet.

'By saying that he would never go back to the island again, but intended to accept an offer he'd had from an Australian university. At the time I took that to mean that he couldn't bear the thought of trying to pick up the pieces and carry on without Eliza, but, thinking about

181

it afterwards, I found something false in that. There were no regrets, he'd sounded really pleased by the prospect of moving back into the world. For the first time, it gave me the idea of turning the situation on its head, or rather turning it the right way up and the moment I did that everything started to fall into place.'

Robin was looking perplexed again, but Toby, who often uses such devices in his plots, caught on at once:

'So now we have Eliza wanting to stay on in the island, even at the cost of sacrificing her husband's career?'

'And paying for it with her life, furthermore, although of course she couldn't have foreseen that and, in the meantime she wanted everything to go on exactly as it was. For the first time ever she feels fulfilled, the biggest star in the firmament, the only one, in fact, needed and adored by everyone around her and with Conrad's undivided attention. Why would she want to exchange all that for a drab existence on the Australian campus?'

'Quite so, but it does seem to me that murdering her was rather a drastic way out of the impasse.'

'He didn't have many options. Clearly, she wouldn't have given him grounds for divorce and, anyway, it wasn't only for that, Toby. He had two other pressing reasons for wanting her out of his life and one was that he was in love with someone else. The second, perhaps even more important, that after her accident Eliza had told him that she could never have any children.'

'Surely he didn't confide this to you over the luncheon table?'

'No, I pieced it together from what Evadne and others had told me, although Conrad did commit one indiscretion, which I'm sure was unintentional. He was telling me about his childhood and how he'd been sent away to a boarding school in England at a tender age. When I asked him if he would do the same with a son of his own, "Oh no, my boy will be brought up in Australia." No "ifs" or "whens", just a statement of fact, as though the boy were already here. It struck an odd note at the time, but I realised afterwards that of course the boy was already here. He's called Ned, furthermore, which should have been a heavy clue for those of us who are familiar with Australian folklore.'

'Oh yes, a sort of Robin Hood character, I believe. Is that the career your parents envisaged for you, Robin?'

'No, I think I was probably named after some friendly bird my mother had taken a liking to. However, since we're on the subject, perhaps I should remind you, Tessa, that you have overlooked one rather important point. Whatever she may, or may not have been told after her accident, Eliza in fact was pregnant when she died.'

'No, I hadn't forgotten and "may or may not" is an accurate way of putting it. Personally, I am convinced that she had not been told anything of the kind, but that it suited her to pretend she had because motherhood was simply not on her agenda and one can well see why. In the first place, any child, particularly a boy, would have been a dangerous rival in her relationship with Conrad. One only had to hear him speak of "his boy" to realise that. Secondly, it really would have meant leaving the island and going back to boring old civilisation. Not even Eliza could have contemplated bringing up a baby in those surroundings, with anything up to a week between themselves and the nearest telephone.'

'Nevertheless, this is just your personal opinion. There is nothing factual, so far as I can see, to support it.'

'Yes, there jolly well is, Robin. Why else did she postpone her flight and decide to stay on for an extra five or six weeks? And why, having done so, did she make such a secret of it? Everyone was mystified by that, but the answer seems perfectly plain to me. She'd realised what was happening to her and her main object in coming here was to get an abortion. Naturally, in the circumstances, she would have allowed plenty of time to arrange matters properly and also to be back in tiptop form by the time she went home.'

'Well yes, given your original premise being right, that would make sense, I admit, but we were given to understand that her main reason for coming was to get some treatment for her back, which in fact is what she set about trying to do the minute she arrived.'

'Only she didn't try very hard, did she? She had an appointment lined up with Alec Henderson, who advised her to spend a few weeks in his clinic and she turned him down flat. That looks to me as though her back trouble was just a blind. It is far more likely that she went straight off to see Alec as soon as she arrived because what she really wanted from him, being so out of touch and unable to ask anyone else, was information of quite a different kind.'

'And now I suppose you mean to confound us both by saying that this is what Alec told Venetia, who passed it on to Ellen?'

'I'd like to, but I have to be honest and the fact is that Alec is far too tight lipped to divulge that kind of thing, even to his angel wife. What he did say, however, which is a pretty good indication, was that Eliza was a very wayward and headstrong young woman. It's so much out of character for him to make a comment of that kind about one of his patients that I'm prepared to accept it as proof that she had offended him deeply by asking for the name and address of the best abortionist in the country.'

'All right, you've made out quite a good case there, so now let's go back to another of your dubious statements. Was your assumption that Conrad was the father of Rosie's child based solely on the fact that he was called Ned?'

'By no means, because I'd already learnt from Rodney

184

that when he ran into Eliza a year or so ago in Sydney, Conrad had gone to the airport to meet a niece or cousin of hers, who was to spend a few months with them at a seaside bungalow they had rented. It is fair to assume, by the way, that this coincided with the offer he'd had from the university, which he was all for accepting, whereas Eliza, who by this time had had a taste of the academic life, was dead set against it.

'The second clue came from Rosie, herself, who passed the remark that while in Australia she had found herself to be pregnant and, as a result, had returned to England, instead of going on to America. I daresay that singly none of these facts would count as evidence in a court of law, but when you put them together and set them against the general background, they do begin to add up. And, after all, no one has ever known who Ned's father was, so why not Conrad? Specially when you remember, as no doubt Toby does with a frisson or two, her claim that she could only fancy a permanent relationship with an older man.'

'Unluckily for her, she picked the wrong one,' Robin said, 'but I am afraid the poor girl must have fallen into the same trap as you and Ellen.'

'Oh, I am sure neither of us could have taken him seriously, you know, even if he hadn't been a criminal. He had a certain style, admittedly, but he was much too self-centred and pleased with himself and too flamboyant for my taste. Imagine the audacity of killing himself in a police car, with a sergeant wedged up beside him!'

'Is that how it happened?'

'So Robin tells me. He was on his way to the station, to help the police in their enquiries, as they put it. No handcuffs, or any of that, but he must have known his number would be up as soon as they caught on to the passport dodge. So while they were circling Hyde Park Corner he pulled out a handkerchief, as though to blow his nose, and swallowed the cyanide that was wrapped inside it.'

'My goodness, that must have brought the traffic to a standstill.'

'He had the reputation of being mean, too, so Tessa tells me, but at least you could say he was careful with the taxpayers' money, just as much as his own,' Robin pointed out.

'Oh yes, indeed, I hadn't thought of that and I am so glad you drew my attention to it. It makes me feel I am not such a bad judge of character, after all.'

'Mrs Parkes is sure to want to know, so before I come to my last question, just tell me what part Brian played in all this. Was he in the game too?'

'Not wittingly, if there is such a word. He was just being used, I'm afraid, but we needn't feel too sorry for him. He was getting free board and lodging and I've no doubt that he did relieve the tedium with a little light pilfering.'

'Although not on the scale that some would have us believe, perhaps?'

'Well, you know, Toby, I'm pretty sure Mrs Parkes made up that tarradiddle about the missing coaster. She was shrewd enough to recognise Rosie right from the start as a disruptive influence and she took immediate action. It was the fluke of finding the coaster again the minute you'd gone to London which didn't quite ring true.'

'You forgot to tell us what Brian was being used for,' Robin reminded me.

'As baby sitter mainly, with first-class qualifications for the job. Naturally, Rosie preferred to cut herself off as far as possible from her family during this stormy period and Brian's presence in her household was enough to ensure that. Also, of course, Roakes was the ideal place to retire to. Right off the map, but still only forty miles from London and less than half that from Windsor, incidentally. So it was very convenient for meetings with her real love, specially if he happened to be driving along a certain main road at a certain time and happened to stop for a lady hitchhiker. But Rosie would never have been able to manage there with Ned, on her own. So Brian was essential to the plan and what tied it all up so neatly was that, knowing his reputation and by fanning its flames, so that the word got around, made it so easy to cast him off when his time was up. Either she would throw him to the police dogs, or else— What was your last question, Toby?'

'I wondered whether she had been provided with the emergency pill too? Somehow, I can't see her using it.'

'Nor can I. She would rely on her fatal charm for the older man to get an acquittal from every judge in the land, but Robin doesn't believe it will come to that and, indeed, why should it? She may or may not have given Conrad Eliza's room number, so that all he had to do was walk up to the desk and ask for the key when she was out. She may or may not have made sure she would be, by making a dinner date for that evening, but none of it could ever be proved. Besides, they are not in themselves criminal acts and who could ever say that she knew what they would lead to?'

'And, perhaps to be fair, she did not. I daresay Conrad was wily enough to con her into believing he was up to some quite different game. I know you'll say I'm sentimental, but I think we should all try hard to believe that.'

'Yes, and why not, Toby? I am sure she will be punished enough, as it is, by everything going so hideously wrong. She must have been wildly in love with him, so one could assume that her heart is now broken, if only temporarily.'

'Quite so, and there is Ned, too, to think of. How very sad for her!'

'A bit sad for Lady Simonson, too, I shouldn't wonder,' Robin said.